"We'll do the best we can."

Toby gently laid the collie on the examining table. The dog was so big that he barely fit. Val noticed that he wasn't wearing a collar. She saw then that a sharp white bone protruded from his mangled left foreleg, and his side was crushed and bleeding. She bit her lip to keep from crying as she handed Doc the instruments he required for his examination.

"X ray first," said Doc. "I'm afraid there are internal injuries as well. I'll try to save the leg, but he needs delicate surgery, and I'm no microsurgeon. Wheel him into the operating room, Mike. We'll do the best we can."

ANIMAL INN

A KID'S BEST FRIEND

Virginia Vail

AN
APPLE
PAPERBACK

SCHOLASTIC INC.
New York Toronto London Auckland Sydney

ISBN 0-590-42787-3

12 11 10 9 8 7   3/9

Printed in the U.S.A.   28

Chapter 1

Valentine Taylor gently pulled back on the reins, slowing the big gray horse from a canter to a trot, then to a walk. The Gray Ghost knew they were heading for home, and he was looking forward to his cozy stall at Animal Inn. He'd have broken into a gallop if Val hadn't held him back. But she knew that since The Ghost didn't see very well, it was dangerous to let him run. He might stumble and fall, and she loved him too much to risk that.

Even though it was fall, the sun was beaming down as if it wanted summer to last as long as possible. Val found it hard to believe that, though she was riding down a little country lane through the rich Pennsylvania farmland, the little town of Essex where the Taylors lived was only a short distance away. She leaned down and patted The Ghost's glossy dappled shoulder. He wasn't sweating at all, in spite of the heat. Val glanced at her watch. It was almost four o'clock — time to take up her duties as her father's assistant in his veterinary practice. Doc had told her that things at Animal Inn were slow today, so she'd had time to ride for a little while after school.

The Ghost snorted and pranced, objecting to Val's pressure on the reins. She knew exactly what he was thinking — oats and hay, and a long drink of fresh, cool water. She herself was looking forward to ice-cold lemonade. She'd made a pitcherful and put it in the refrigerator in Animal Inn's treatment room. She could almost taste it now!

As Val and The Ghost ambled into the stable yard next to the Large Animal Clinic, she saw Animal Inn's vet van pulling out of the parking lot. Mike Strickler, Doc Taylor's elderly assistant who took care of the animals after office hours, was driving. And it looked as though Toby Curran, one of Doc's young helpers, was sitting beside him. Where were they going? Val wondered. Toby was supposed to be helping Doc until she returned. Maybe they were going to pick up a sick animal somewhere.

Val dismounted, rubbed The Ghost down, and led him into his stall. She poked her head into the treatment room. Her father was examining a very large black-and-white cat which was yowling at the top of its lungs.

"Where's Toby?" she asked.

Dr. Taylor, one hand firmly holding down the cat, glanced up at his daughter. "Mike's driving him in the van to pick up an injured dog. Toby was biking back to Animal Inn when he saw a car hit the dog. Vallie, check with Pat, will you? She wants to leave early today, so you'll have to take over the reception desk."

Val nodded and scooted into the reception area. Pat Dempwolf, Animal Inn's receptionist, bounced out of her chair the minute she saw Val.

"Oh, Val, I'm so glad to see you! My little grand-daughter has the flu, and my daughter has to go to the drugstore to pick up her medicine. She's been waiting for me to baby-sit. Now where's my purse?" Pat bent down and fumbled under the counter that separated the reception desk from the waiting room and came up with her pocketbook. "Tell Doc not to worry, I'll be in tomorrow right on time."

"I will," Val said. "I hope Tiffany gets better."

"Thanks! 'Bye-bye!"

Pat hurried out, and Val took her place behind the desk. The phone rang immediately.

"Good afternoon, Animal Inn. May I help you?" she said, then listened as the caller described how one of his cows had gotten tangled up in some barbed wire. Could Doc come to the Hess farm later this afternoon? Val said she'd give Doc the message and made careful notes on the message pad. Then she turned to the only person in the waiting room, a

3

woman with a big German shepherd.

"Hi, Mrs. Starner. Is Fritz here for his shots?" she asked.

"That's right. Will we have to wait long, Val?"

"I don't think so," said Val. "Dad's taking care of Blackie Fredericks right now, but he ought to be finished soon." She came out from behind the desk and patted Fritz.

"Give Val your paw, Fritz," said Mrs. Starner. Fritz did, and Mrs. Starner smiled proudly as Val solemnly shook it. "That's his only trick," she confided. "But what I say is, tricks are all right for *little* dogs. *Big* dogs would just feel silly, wouldn't you, Fritz?"

Fritz wagged his tail and smiled a dog smile, and Val smiled back. But her mind wasn't really on Fritz. She was thinking about the dog that had been hit by the car. Where were Toby and Mike? They should be back soon. She went to the front window and peered out. How could anybody just drive away and leave a poor, injured animal by the side of the road? How could anybody be so careless as to hit it in the first place?

She thought about her own two dogs. Well, they weren't exactly *her* dogs — they belonged to the whole family. But they were both very precious to Val, and the thought of either Sunshine, the big golden re-

4

triever, or Jocko, the little shaggy black-and-white mongrel, being hit by a car upset her very much. She knew she shouldn't let herself get so emotional over hurt animals. If she was going to be a vet like her father, she'd have to learn to control her reactions. But it was hard to be professional when an animal's life was at stake.

Val's heart ached for any animal that was ill or in pain. She thought about The Ghost, her very own horse. His previous owner had been ready to destroy him because The Ghost was going blind and would never be a championship jumper again. Val had spent just about every cent she had saved to buy him, and had saved his life. And she hadn't regretted it, not for one single second! And neither, she was sure, had The Ghost.

But what about the dog? Where on earth was the van?

Just then she saw it coming down Orchard Lane, and Val ran to open the front door. The van screeched to a stop, and Mike Strickler scrambled out. He flung open the side door of the van, and Toby emerged, staggering under the weight of a huge collie. The dog lay limp in his arms, its gold-and-white fur stained with blood.

Val gasped and stood aside as Toby came in with his burden. Toby's usually cheerful face was grim, his brown hair falling over his worried eyes.

"Oh, the poor thing!" cried Mrs. Starner. "Is he dead?" Fritz began to bark.

"Not yet," Toby mumbled.

"Pretty near, though," said Mike, trotting right behind Toby. "Some folks oughta be put in jail, that's what I say! Folks that drive fancy sports cars and hit poor dumb animals and keep right on goin'. They oughta be *shot*, that's what I say!"

At that moment Doc came out of the treatment room with Mr. Fredericks and Blackie, saying, "Vallie, I told Mr. Fredericks we'd send him a bill for Blackie's treatment. Leave a note for Pat to bill him next month." He took one look at the collie in Toby's arms and added, "Bring him right in, Toby. Mrs. Starner, I'm sorry, but you'll have to wait a little longer. This is an emergency."

"Well, I can see that, all right," said Mrs. Starner. "Fritz won't mind, will you, Fritz? That poor dog looks like a goner. But if anyone can save him, you can, Doc."

"Thanks, Mrs. Starner," Doc said. He went into the treatment room, followed by Toby and the collie, with Val and Mike trailing behind. Val silently agreed with Mrs. Starner. If it was possible to help the injured animal, Doc could do it. After all, Val thought, he was the best vet in Essex, Pennsylvania — maybe in the whole world! But what if the dog were already

6

dead? He wasn't moving at all. It didn't look as if he was even breathing!

Toby gently laid the collie on the examining table. The dog was so big that he barely fit. Val noticed that he wasn't wearing a collar. She saw then that a sharp white bone protruded from his mangled left foreleg, and his side was crushed and bleeding. She bit her lip to keep from crying as she handed Doc the instruments he required for his examination.

"X-ray first," said Doc. "I'm afraid there are internal injuries as well. I'll try to save the leg, but he needs delicate surgery, and I'm no microsurgeon. Wheel him into the operating room, Mike. We'll do the best we can."

"Is there anything I can do?" asked Toby anxiously.

"Afraid not, Toby," Doc said. "You'd better go on home. We'll be here for a while yet. Vallie, please call Mrs. Racer and tell her we're going to be late."

"If it's all the same to you, I'd like to hang around a while — see how he is," Toby mumbled. He looked down at his bloodstained shirt. "Guess I'd better rinse this out, or Mom'll have a fit when she sees me."

While Toby washed his shirt in the treatment room sink, Val phoned the Taylors' housekeeper and delivered the message.

"Guess I'll go ahead and give Teddy and Erin their supper," said Mrs. Racer. "Sounds like you're

7

going to be a while. Now don't you get all upset, Vallie, you hear? I'll keep dinner for you and Doc nice and hot in the oven."

"Thanks, Mrs. Racer," Val said. The thought of eating anything at all made her feel sick. How could she eat when a poor animal was suffering so?

She hung up the phone and hurried into the operating room. Would Doc have to amputate the collie's leg? What a terrible thought! But if it would save the dog's life, it would be worth it. Val had seen other animals who made do with only three legs. The important thing was that the dog would live.

"I don't know. I just don't know," Doc sighed later as he and Val came out of the operating room. He'd set the leg and had administered an antibiotic to guard against possible infection, as well as a shot of painkiller. Doc had found that the fractured ribs had not pierced any vital organs, but the collie had lost a lot of blood and was very weak. He was now in Animal Inn's intensive care unit, and Mike had received instructions to keep a close eye on him and to call Doc at home if the animal seemed to be getting worse.

Val couldn't restrain her tears. "He's going to die, Dad, isn't he?"

Doc shook his head. "I hope not, but I can't

8

make any promises. He's in pretty bad shape, and at the moment I'm pretty low on miracles."

"And his owner doesn't even know what happened to him!" said Val softly. "If only he was wearing a collar with a name tag! We don't even know what to call him!"

Doc put his arms around her and hugged her close. Val pressed her tear-stained face against the shoulder of his white lab coat. Somehow, just having her father hold her made her feel a little better. Doc didn't have to say anything. Val knew he understood exactly how she felt, because he felt the same way. Only he didn't let it show, the way she did. Somewhere, she was sure, somebody was wondering where his pet was, worrying about why he hadn't come home. The dog's owner must be frantic.

"Well, guess we'd better be getting home," said Doc gruffly. He rubbed his bearded chin against the top of Val's head. "If you're going to be a vet when you grow up, honey, you have to realize that all you can do is your best. We've done our best. Now we just have to wait and see." Releasing her, he added, "Just let me wash up and we'll be on our way."

"Dad. . . ." Val followed him to the sink. "I don't suppose you'd let me sleep here tonight? I could use the cot Mike keeps in the back room. If anything goes wrong, I'd be right here to help out."

Doc shook his head. "No way, Vallie. You have school tomorrow, and homework to do tonight. Mike will keep us posted."

"I knew you were going to say that." Handing him a towel, Val sighed. "But if he wakes up all alone in a strange place, he'll be scared. I could talk to him, tell him not to be afraid. . . ."

"Vallie, I said no, and I mean *no*. It's been a long day. Time to go home."

They went into the waiting room . . . and saw Mrs. Starner sitting there with Fritz, talking to Toby.

Doc gave Val a rueful glance. "We'll go home *after* I tend to Fritz. Sorry, Mrs. Starner. Bring Fritz right in."

"Oh, and Dad, I forgot to tell you — Mr. Hess called. One of his cows got tangled up in some barbed wire and needs her cuts tended to. I told him you'd call," Val said.

"Call him back and tell him that if it's not an emergency, to put some antiseptic on the scrapes and I'll be over first thing tomorrow morning," Doc said.

It was more than half an hour later that Doc, Val, and Toby left Animal Inn, heading for the van. It was getting dark and there was a chill in the air.

"Mike's right," said Toby. "Hit-and-run drivers oughta be shot!"

"If that dog was a person, we could call the

police," Val said. "They'd put out an all-points bulletin, like they do on all the TV shows. But he's only an animal, so no APB's. Nobody will do a single thing! It's not fair!"

"You're right, Vallie," Doc said. "It isn't fair, but that's the way it is. All we can do is try to save the lives of the unfortunate victims." He turned to Toby. "Toby, how about a lift? Your mom's going to be worried about you."

"That's okay," said Toby. "I gave her a call — told her I'd be late. And it's so far out of your way. . . ."

"Don't be silly," Val said. "Stow your bike in the back of the van. Besides, we have to talk."

"What about?" asked Toby as he hefted his bright blue ten-speed into the van. He hadn't known Val very long, but it was long enough to know that when she got that gleam in her eye, she had a project in mind. Like when she'd decided to buy The Gray Ghost.

Doc revved the engine and Val and Toby piled in beside him. "Yes, Vallie, what about?" Doc asked, driving out of the parking lot. "What's on your mind?"

"That dog, that's what!" cried Val. "I can't just sit around twiddling my thumbs while a *murderer* gets off scot-free!"

"The dog's still alive," Doc reminded her.

"Just barely," Val shot back. Her grief had been

replaced by anger, and she was ready to do battle. "Suppose he was a person — suppose somebody had run a *person* down! The police would need to know everything the eyewitness saw. And that's you, Toby. You saw the whole thing, didn't you?"

"Well, yeah, kind of," Toby admitted.

"Then pretend I'm a cop. Tell me absolutely everything you remember about the accident." Val fumbled in her knapsack and pulled out a notebook and pencil. "What did you see?"

"Well. . . ." Toby scrunched up his face, thinking hard. "I was riding my bike along the York Road because I'd just delivered some medicine to Mr. Beemer's farm for his sick calf. . . ."

"What time was that?" Val asked.

"About quarter to four, I guess. And all of a sudden I see this great-looking car — a white Corvette! Man, it was one neat car!" Toby leaned forward, caught up in his memory of the moment. "It must have been going at least sixty-five. And then all of a sudden, this dog runs across the road. The car swerves, but it doesn't stop. It hits the dog and knocks him into the field beside the road, and then it just keeps right on going! So I pull over on my bike, and I go over to the dog, and I see he's really hurt bad. He's bleeding a lot and he's not moving, except for his tail — his tail's wagging just a little." Toby shivered. "It was awful! I knew I couldn't bring him back to Animal Inn on my bike, so I rode as fast as I could, and told Doc. Mike had just arrived, so he drove me back. We picked up the dog and put him in the van . . . and you know the rest.''

Val shivered, too. "Yes, I know the rest. Did you see the license plate of the car?''

"Yeah, it was a Pennsylvania plate. One of the ones that spells out a word or a name. Something like CLOUD or something. I'd never seen that car before. But I'd recognize it if I saw it again. I'm positive of that!'' Toby said.

Val finished scribbling her notes. "Great! Now all we have to do is find the owner of the car!''

Doc looked over at her. "Vallie, do you know how many cars there are in Essex and the surrounding countryside?''

"Sure,'' said Val. "But how many of those cars are white Corvettes with special license plates? I'm going to find the owner of that car, and Toby's going to help me. Between the two of us, we'll track him down one way or another!''

"That's nuts!'' Toby said flatly.

"That's what you said when I told you I was going to buy The Ghost, remember?'' Val shot back. "But I did buy him, and now he's mine! That poor dog is lying back there at Animal Inn, maybe dead by now. Whoever hit him has to know what he's done. Maybe we can't get the police to put him in jail, but at least he'll think twice before he runs down another dog — or cat, or *person*!" She turned from Toby to her father. "You understand, don't you, Dad?"

Doc reached over and squeezed Val's knee. "Yes, honey, I do."

Toby sighed. "I know when I'm beat. What do you want me to do?"

"I want you to check around the farms, just like I'm going to do in town," she said. "Ask questions, check license plates, keep your eyes open for that white Corvette. If you find it, you call me right away, and if *I* find it, I'll call *you*. And then we'll go right up to that person and tell him what he's done, and make sure he never does it again!"

"Just a minute, Vallie," Doc said sternly. "I want it clearly understood that if either you or Toby do locate the car and its driver, you are not to do *any-thing* without checking with me first, okay?"

"Yes, sir," Toby said.

"Especially you, Vallie."

"Yes, Dad, I promise," Val said.

"Good," said Doc. "And one other thing. What about trying to find the owner of the dog? It seems to me that should be your first priority."

"Oh, Dad, you're right! I'll make a lot of signs tonight — Erin can help me. I'll put them up all over town tomorrow before school. Toby, can you make some signs, too? And be sure you put down the phone

14

number of Animal Inn. . . . Oh, dear. . . ." Val's voice trailed off.

"What is it?" asked Doc.

"Well, what if the dog's owner sees a sign and calls, and the dog is dead?" she whispered. "Maybe it would be better if he didn't know."

"I think he'd want to know, Vallie," Doc said. "Sometimes it's better to know the worst than to keep on hoping. Then you can begin to accept it and try to go on with your life."

Like when Mom died, Val thought. When her mother had been killed three years ago in an automobile accident, it was the worst thing that had ever happened. The pain would never completely go away, but as time went by, it was easier to bear. And there were so many happy memories of her mother. . . .

"I'll help you, Val," Toby said. "But even if we do find the dog's owner, I bet we'll never find that car. It could be in another state by now. If we *do* find the driver, though, I personally would very much like to punch him out!"

"You know something, Toby?" said Doc. "So would I! But I won't," he added hastily, "and neither will you. Remember, no going off half-cocked, making a bad situation worse."

"We won't, Dad," Val told him, and Toby agreed. But somehow, Val knew she had to find a way to make the hit-and-run driver pay for what he'd done.

Chapter
2

"But Val, I can't, and you can't, either!" said Jill Dearborne, Val's best friend, as they headed for their lockers after school the next day. "We have a meeting of the Harvest Dance Committee in five minutes! I'm the chairman — I can't just cancel the meeting because you want me to bike all over town looking for a white Corvette. And you're head of the refreshment committee. How would it look if we both didn't show up? You know what'll happen. Lila Bascombe will take over the whole thing and turn it into a hearts-and-flowers *mess*! I'll do it afterward, but you have to come and back me up at the meeting."

Val sighed. "Oh, all right. But the dance isn't nearly as important as finding out who ran down that poor collie. Keep it short, okay?"

"Lila really drives me up the wall lately," said Jill. "I take that back. She's *always* driven me up the wall, only it's gotten worse since she started hanging out with all those ninth-graders. To hear her talk, you'd think she and Jeff Willard were practically engaged! That's why she wants the dance to be formal. She's dying to get all dressed up and slow-dance with Jeff all night."

"I don't own a formal gown," Val said. "And even if I did, I can't think of anything worse than dancing with some boy who barely comes up to my chin! I'm *yards* taller than any of the boys in our class."

"Well, you know Lila. She's been boy-crazy since kindergarten," said Jill. "And that's why you have to come to the meeting. No heart-shaped balloons and fancy dresses. Just good, old-fashioned fun and plenty of cider and homemade cookies and stuff. Mrs. Racer's going to bake, isn't she?"

"She sure is," Val said. "She's already started. But you *will* come with me when the meeting's over, won't you? I just have to find the person who hit that dog!"

"How is he?" Jill asked as they walked down the hall to the library where the meeting was to be held. Tiny, delicate and blonde, Jill was a complete contrast to Val, who was tall, auburn-haired, and broad-shouldered, a feminine version of Doc Taylor.

"Not so great," Val said. "I called Dad at lunch. He said the dog was holding his own, but barely. Oh, I hope Rex's owner sees the notices I put up this morning! If Rex were my dog, I'd be worried to death."

"Rex?" Jill repeated. "I thought you didn't know what his name was."

"We don't. But I can't just keep calling him 'dog.' He's beautiful and kind of kingly, so I thought Rex would be a good name for him until we find out what his real name is."

"Poor Rex," sighed Jill. "I promise I'll keep the meeting short. And then we'll bike all over Essex. Between you and me and Toby, I bet we'll find that car!"

"I sure hope so," Val said. "And I hope Rex's owner finds him — before it's too late."

An hour later, Val and Jill were mounting their bikes in front of Alexander Hamilton Junior High. They'd managed to prevent Lila and her friends from taking over, and the Harvest Dance was firmly established. No formal gowns, and lots of recorded rock music. Lila had pouted and complained, but Miss Becker, the teacher in charge, had insisted that she go along with the majority. Lila had left in a huff, which was just fine with Jill and Val.

"You ready?" Val asked Jill. "Let's go! I'll take Market Street and Beaver Street and all the streets in between. You take Princess and King. I'll meet you at five o'clock in front of Schaeffer's Sporting Goods and we'll compare notes."

"You're on," said Jill. "But I have to be home by five-thirty. I have a history test tomorrow, and I have to study like crazy."

Val's legs ached. She'd pedaled all over Essex, checking every car in sight. Her heart ached, too. None of them was a white Corvette with a license place that spelled out CLOUD. Now she was waiting in front of Schaeffer's, waiting for Jill to show up. Maybe Jill had had better luck. She certainly hoped so!

Maybe Doc was right. Maybe it was impossible to find the car that had hit Rex. Toby had said that it might be in another state by now, and she had to admit it might be true. But she couldn't give up. She *wouldn't* give up, not until she was absolutely certain there was no hope.

Dusk was falling when Jill came into view. She got off her bike, and Val could tell at once that her friend had had no more success than she.

"No luck," Jill said. "I didn't see a single car that matched your description. And I have a dentist appointment after school tomorrow, so I can't go with you then."

"Thanks, anyway," said Val sadly. "I really appreciate you helping me out. I guess we'd both better be getting home."

The two girls rode down Main Street. When they

reached Jill's block, she turned off with a silent wave, and Val continued riding alone. As she passed the houses on her way, warm, golden light streaming from their windows, she wondered if maybe inside one of them, someone was worrying about a lost pet. She thought of Rex. How had he gotten through the day? Had anyone seen her signs and called Animal Inn to claim him?

Val turned down Old Mill Road and a few minutes later pulled into the driveway beside the Taylors' big stone house. She hopped off her bike, wheeled it into the garage, and was heading for the front door when she saw a small figure trotting down the street. As the figure passed under a street lamp, she saw it was her little brother, Teddy. He saw her, too, and began to run, clutching his stomach. Val paused, concerned. Was Teddy sick?

But when he dashed up the path and met her by the door, she saw that he was grinning, and his brown eyes, beneath the Phillies baseball cap he always wore, were sparkling with excitement.

"Vallie, guess what!" he said. "Guess what I've got!"

"A tummy-ache?" Val joked.

"No, dopey!" He carefully unzipped his jacket partway and moved into the light of the lamp over the door. "Look!"

Val peered into the opening. Two beady eyes

looked at her from a furry, pointed face.

"What is it?" she asked, fascinated.

"It's a ferret! Isn't he neat? My friend Eric gave him to me. Go on, pat him. He doesn't bite. He's real friendly. Eric says ferrets make the best pets in the world."

Val stroked the sleek little brown head with one finger. "He *is* neat," she agreed. "Bring him inside and let's take a look at him."

"You better go first and get Jocko and Sunshine out of the way," Teddy said. "I don't think dogs and ferrets get along too good — not at first, anyway. But they'll be real good friends after a while."

Val let herself in and was immediately pounced upon by both happy dogs. After she'd petted them, and taken off her jacket, Val called over the noise of their barking to Erin, who was curled up on the sofa reading one of her favorite ballet books. "Erin, put the dogs in the backyard, will you? Teddy's waiting to come in."

Eleven-year-old Erin glanced up, a puzzled expression on her face. "Why can't he come in if the dogs are here?"

"Because he's got a ferret," Val said. "Come on, Erin — *move!*"

"He's got a *what?*"

"A ferret. It's a little animal. He's afraid the dogs will go after it."

21

Erin obediently put down her book and stood up, grabbing Jocko and Sunshine. She dragged them both toward the back door.

Val sniffed the air. Something smelled delicious. Mrs. Racer must have baked a cake, or maybe more cookies for the dance.

The front door opened a crack and Teddy stuck his head in. "All clear?" he asked.

"Yep. Come on in."

Teddy did. The ferret's sleek head darted this way and that out of its cozy nest in Teddy's jacket. It had an amazingly long neck, and its fur was a glossy, sable brown. Its bright eyes peered out from a darker brown mask, kind of like a skinny raccoon. Val fell in love with it at once, as she did with any animal she came in contact with.

"Can I hold it?" Val asked.

Teddy nodded. "Sure. But he's *mine*, Vallie, and don't you forget it! I want him to love *me* best."

Val lifted the slender animal out of Teddy's jacket. It rubbed its head against her chin, and she giggled. She'd never actually handled a ferret before, though she'd read about them in books.

"He's great, Teddy," she said, nuzzling nose-to-nose with the little creature. "You said Eric gave him to you? Why?"

" 'Cause his mom didn't like it. She says it looks like a furry snake with legs."

Teddy reached out his hands and Val reluctantly handed him the ferret. It scrambled up his chest and wrapped itself around his neck. It reminded Val of her grandmother's fur piece. The ferret looked like a mink, long and sinuous, with small, delicate paws and a smooth, fine-boned head.

"Does Dad know about him?" she asked. "You know the rules. Whenever we want a new pet, we have to ask Dad first. And then we all have to agree."

"Well. . . ." Teddy shucked off his jacket and stroked the ferret's fur. "I don't *think* so."

"What do you mean, you don't think so?"

"Well, Eric only gave him to me today, so I didn't have time to check with Dad," Teddy said. "But he's such a super ferret, I'm absolutely sure Dad will say it's okay."

"Is that the ferret?" asked Erin, running in from the kitchen. "Oh, it's adorable! What's its name?"

"Frank," Teddy said.

"Frank?" Val echoed. "That's a weird name for an animal."

"No it's not," said Teddy. "Eric named him after Major Frank Burns on *M*A*S*H*. You know — Ferret-face?"

"I love it!" Erin cried. "And I bet Daddy will love it, too. Where is Daddy, anyway?"

"Doc had to go to the Steppler farm. Mr. Steppler's goats have some kind of ailment so he went to take a look at them," said Mrs. Racer, coming into the living room. She tucked a stray strand of silvery hair neatly beneath her white lawn prayer covering. Mrs. Racer was a Mennonite and always wore a little white cap on her head, along with her simple print dresses in the Mennonite style. A spotless white apron covered her lavender dress. "He'll be home in about half an hour. . . . *What's that?*"

She had just seen the ferret wrapped around Teddy's neck. Her pale blue eyes widened. "That's a *weasel!*" she cried. "Teddy Taylor, what're you doing with a weasel?"

"It's not a weasel, Mrs. Racer. It's a ferret," Teddy said. "He's my new pet."

"It's a weasel," Mrs. Racer said, "and weasels are terrible animals! They're killers, that's what they are! They eat chickens and suck the innards out of eggs!"

"It's *not* a weasel," Val said. "Ferrets are different. They belong to the same family as weasels, but they don't do all the bad things weasels do. Teddy's friend Eric gave it to him. I'm sure he won't be destructive. And all our eggs are in the refrigerator so he couldn't possibly suck out their innards."

"Them weasels can open refrigerator doors," Mrs. Racer said darkly. "And they eat everything in sight. M'son Henry has a chicken farm and he's told me what them weasels do. They have real sharp

24

teeth — bite off a chicken's head just like that!" She snapped her fingers.

Right at that moment, Frank opened his mouth in a wide yawn. Sure enough, he displayed an impressive set of sharp little teeth.

"Wow!" said Erin, backing away. "Maybe you ought to put him down, Teddy. What if he decides you're a big chicken, and takes a big bite out of *you*?"

"Gimme a break!" Teddy groaned. "Ferrets are smart. They know the difference between chickens and people. Do I look like a chicken? Huh? Do I?"

"They go after rabbits, too," Mrs. Racer said. "What about Vallie's bunny rabbits out by the garage? And Archie — a weasel'd nip off a duck's foot like you'd chop the top off a carrot."

"Mrs. Racer, Frank isn't a weasel," Val said again. "And even if he was, Archie and the rabbits are perfectly safe in their pen. Why don't you pat him? He's soft and furry, just like a cat. Go on, touch him," she urged.

"Me touch a thieving, murdering weasel? No-sirree!" Mrs. Racer scowled at the little animal. "Just you wait till Doc gets home! Then we'll see what's what!" She bustled off to the kitchen, muttering under her breath, "Weasels! Well, I never!"

"I don't know, Teddy," said Erin. "Maybe Mrs. Racer's right. Maybe Frank *is* a weasel. Maybe you ought to give him back."

25

"Erin, go jump in the lake!" Teddy grumbled. "I can't give him back. Eric's mother said 'no way.' She wanted to let him loose out in the country, and that's what she'll do if I can't keep him."

"We can't let that happen," Val said. She carefully lifted Frank from Teddy's shoulder and snuggled him under her chin. "I read an article about ferrets in the *Gazette* the other day. These people have a ferret farm outside of town. They breed them for pets, and they said that if you let them loose, they'll die in a few days. The article said ferrets are becoming very popular pets. Just look at Frank. Does he look like a killer?"

Frank's long, slender body wriggled in Val's arms, and he rubbed his pointy face against her neck.

"Well, I guess he's kinda cute," Erin admitted. "But those teeth. . . ."

Rrrow?

Cleveland, Val's big orange cat, came into the living room and began weaving around Val's legs.

"Let's see what Cleveland thinks about him," Val suggested. She knelt down and put Frank on the floor. Since Frank's legs were much shorter than Cleveland's, the ferret had to stretch his long neck way up in order to come nose-to-nose with the cat. Cleveland's whiskers twitched as he sniffed at the strange creature.

Suddenly Frank rolled over onto his back, stick-

26

ing all four little feet up in the air. Cleveland carefully sniffed him all over. Then Cleveland stalked off, obviously satisfied that the ferret wasn't another cat and presented no threat to Cleveland's position in the Taylor household. Frank stood up and slunk across the rug to Teddy. Teddy bent over and picked him up.

"He already knows who his master is!" Teddy said proudly.

"What do ferrets eat?" Erin asked.

"Anything," Teddy told her. "Eric used to feed him dry cat food. Frank's housebroken, too. He uses a litter box, just like Cleveland."

"If Dad says you can keep him, he'll have to have his own litter box," said Val. "I don't think Cleveland would want to share his."

"In *my* room," Teddy said. "Frank's going to be *my* ferret. I bet he'll get along great with my hamsters."

Erin suddenly ran to the front window. "Daddy's home!" she cried. "He just pulled into the driveway."

Rex! Val thought guiltily. Teddy's ferret had made her forget all about the injured collie. She hurried to open the door.

"Dad, how's Rex doing?" she asked as her father came in.

"Holding his own, Vallie," Doc said, giving her

a quick kiss. "It's lucky he's such a big, strong dog. He just might make it. But the leg doesn't look good. I'm afraid I may have to amputate."

Val caught her breath in dismay as Erin and Teddy, still clutching Frank, came over to hug their father.

"Did anybody call about him?" Val asked. "I put up lots of signs."

"No, not a single call. . . ." Doc suddenly saw the ferret. "Where did *that* come from?"

"Eric gave him to me," Teddy said. "It's a ferret. His name's Frank. I can keep him, can't I? Please?"

"It's a weasel, that's what it is," said Mrs. Racer, coming into the living room. The honk of a car horn sounded outside, and she took off her apron and handed it to Erin while Teddy ran to get her coat.

"That's m'son Henry," Mrs. Racer said. "Mark my words, Doc, you'll be sorry if you take a weasel into this house!"

After she had left, the Taylors headed for the kitchen. Erin had laid four places at the butcher block table.

"Mrs. Racer doesn't understand ferrets," Teddy said, sitting down at his place next to Doc. "She says Frank's a killer. But he's not. He's just a nice, cuddly ferret. I *can* keep him, can't I?"

"I'll have to think about it, son," said Doc. "Why did Eric give him to you?"

28

"Eric's mom's kind of like Mrs. Racer. She says Frank gives her the creeps. She wanted Eric to turn him loose out in the country. But Vallie says he'd die out there all by himself. And I can't let that happen to good old Frank!"

While Teddy told Doc more about the ferret, Val began serving the stew Mrs. Racer had prepared. Since Val didn't eat meat, there was also a vegetable casserole for her. Doc told Teddy to put Frank in the pantry while they ate. Val hoped Doc would say that Teddy could keep him. It would be nice to have a ferret in the family.

But her thoughts kept coming back to Rex. She wondered if Toby had had better luck than she and Jill at locating the white car. Val tried very hard not to think about Rex's leg. She knew that Doc would only amputate if he had no other choice. And the dog's owner, she was sure, would love him just as much with three legs as when he had four.

After supper, Val phoned Toby.

"Nothing," he told her. "I made those signs like I said I would, and I put them up around school and stuck some in mailboxes. I got my brothers to help look for the car, too, but no dice. I guess Doc told you nobody called about the dog, either."

"Yes, he did," Val sighed. "I just can't understand it. If Jocko or Sunshine ran away, I'd be looking all over for them! Oh, Toby," she added, "are you working at Animal Inn tomorrow after school?"

"No — I was supposed to have basketball practice but Coach Brubaker canceled it. Why?"

"I was wondering if maybe you'd help me look around Essex for the car. Jill went with me today, but she has a dentist appointment tomorrow. Could you meet me at Hamilton after school on your bike? We could split up the way Jill and I did and cover a lot more ground than I could alone."

"Yeah, I guess I could do that," Toby said. "Around three-thirty, okay?"

"That's great!" said Val. "Thanks so much. We'll find it, I know we will!"

"I hope you're right," Toby said. "But what if the guy's from Pittsburgh, or Altoona, or somewhere? It was a Pennsylvania license plate, but Pennsylvania's a pretty big state."

"Yes, I know. But we have to try. See you tomorrow, Toby. And thanks again. I really mean it."

"No big deal. . . . Hey, Val, did I tell you that my little brother Jake's going to enter Harvey and her babies in the next 4-H fair?" Toby asked suddenly. Harvey was Jake's rabbit. In spite of the name, Harvey had turned out to be a doe and had given birth to six healthy babies.

"That's great, Toby," said Val. "What did Jake name them?"

"Well, there's Tarzan, and Jane, and Captain

Marvel, and The Hulk — he's the fattest one — and Doc, after your father, and — " Toby paused for effect " — and Valentine. Val for short."

Val grinned. "Your brother named one of his rabbits after me? Gee, that's neat! I never had an animal named after me before!"

"It was my idea," Toby admitted. Val could just see his ears turning red the way they always did when he was embarrassed. "There's just one thing. . . . We're not exactly sure that Valentine's a girl. It's kind of hard to tell with rabbits."

"It sure is," Val said with a giggle. "But I don't care one way or the other. Tell Jake thanks for me. 'Night, Toby."

" 'Night, Val."

Chapter
3

"I talked to Toby last night," Val told Jill when they met the following day before their first class. "He hasn't seen the car. And nobody's called Animal Inn about Rex, either. Dad's probably going to have to amputate Rex's leg."

"That's awful!" Jill shuddered. "But if it'll save his life. . . ."

"That's what I'm hoping," said Val. "Toby's coming with me this afternoon to look for the car. I'm supposed to be working for Dad after school, but he gave me the afternoon off." She sighed. "That means I won't be able to see Rex — or The Ghost. The Ghost probably won't even remember me. I haven't been out there for two whole days!"

"Oh, Val, don't be silly," Jill said. "Of course he will. I'm glad Toby's coming with you. Believe me, I'd much rather be going, too, instead of sitting in Dr. Adams's chair while he attacks my cavities with that drill!"

The girls started down the hall to their math class.

"I think this time you ought to check out the really rich neighborhoods," Jill continued. "Like Wyndham Heights. Those people are more likely to own a fancy sports car."

"I was thinking the same thing," Val said. "We'll go there first thing."

"Val. . . ." Jill paused, then said, "If you find the driver of that car — "

"*When* I find him," Val corrected.

"Okay, when you find him, what're you going to do?"

Val frowned. "I'm not really sure. Dad made me promise not to do anything without talking to him first, so I won't. All I know is, I can't let that hit-and-run driver get away with it. It's his fault if Rex loses his leg!"

"If Rex was a person, he could sue," Jill said. "But he's only a dog."

"Yes," Val said sadly. "Only a dog. . . ."

She was so wrapped up in her thoughts about Rex that she wasn't looking where she was going. She bumped into Lila Bascombe, who was heading in the opposite direction with her friends Courtney and Kimberly. Lila's books and notebook fell on the floor. Lila was furious.

"Val Taylor, you're the clumsiest girl I ever met!" Lila fumed. "Why don't you look where you're going?"

Val gritted her teeth. "Sorry, Lila. It was an ac-

33

cident." She picked up Lila's belongings and shoved them at her. "Here."

"Thanks *so* much!" Lila glared at her, then at Jill. "But what else can you expect from people who want to turn the Harvest Dance into a children's party? And I guess you want *my* decoration committee to put cornstalks and cute scarecrows and silly stuff like that all over the gym, Jill. It's going to be so tacky I just might not come at all!"

"Well, Lila, if that's the way you feel, I'm sure you wouldn't be missed," Jill said sweetly.

Wish I'd said that, Val thought. She knew she wasn't really clumsy, but Lila always made her feel as if she was. Lila was always putting people down. She was the most unpleasant person Val had ever met.

The bell sounded for classes to begin. Lila, followed by her two friends (all three with noses in the air), swept past Val and Jill.

"The princess of Hamilton Junior High!" Jill growled. "She gives me a pain where a pill can't reach!"

"Me, too," Val said. "Come on — we're going to be late for math."

Val had a conference with her history teacher after school, so she barely made it to the bike rack by half past three. As she unlocked her bike, she saw

Toby pedaling toward her down College Avenue. She waved and Toby waved back. He pulled up next to her.

"Three-thirty on the dot," he said, checking his watch. "You ready?"

"Sure am. Let's go!"

Val was mounting her bike when Lila came out of the main entrance and down the steps. Much to Val's surprise, Lila walked over to her and Toby, a big smile on her face.

"Hi, Val," Lila said brightly. "Just wanted to tell you how great you did in gym this afternoon. You're really a whiz at volleyball!"

Val stared at her and finally managed to mutter, "Thanks."

What had gotten into Lila? She'd never before said one nice thing about Val, either to her face or behind her back. Now here she was, being super-friendly. Val remembered something Mrs. Racer said when somebody was being suspiciously nice: "Butter wouldn't melt in her mouth." Val could almost see butter between Lila's teeth! What was going on?

Lila turned to Toby, fluttering her long, dark lashes, and then Val understood. As Jill had said, Lila was boy-crazy, and she'd obviously decided that Toby looked interesting. Toby? Val stifled a giggle. Toby was like a big brother!

"I'm absolutely hopeless at sports," Lila was say-

35

ing to Toby. "Not like Val. Val's so — so *big* and *strong*, and such a jock. Softball, basketball, volleyball, you name it. If it's a game with a ball, she's good at it."

She makes me sound like an overgrown puppy! Val thought.

"It looks like Val isn't going to introduce us," Lila went on. "I'm Lila Bascombe. Val and I are in the same homeroom. Who are you?"

"Toby Curran. Hi," said Toby. He looked uncomfortable.

"Curran? Of Curran's Dairy?" Lila asked, making her eyes big and wide. "I just *love* Curran's ice cream!"

"Yeah, that's my dad." Toby looked at Val. "We ought to get moving. I have to be home by six."

"Right!" Val replied quickly. " 'Bye, Lila. See you around."

"I hope I'll see *you* around," Lila said to Toby. It was as if Val had suddenly disappeared.

"Yeah . . . right. Nice meeting you." Toby started off on his bike and Val pedaled after him, taking the lead.

"Where are we going?" Toby asked after they had been riding for a while. They had passed through the center of town and were now coming to the more exclusive residential district of Essex.

"We're near Wyndham Heights," Val told him

over her shoulder. "The people who live here are more likely to own a car like the one that hit Rex."

She told him what streets to cover while she took the ones she was familiar with. They split up, agreeing to meet at Willard Park an hour later.

Not long after four-thirty, Val pedaled wearily into the little park and dropped her bike on the grass. She stretched out under a big maple tree, staring up into the golden leaves overhead. Her legs were aching. She'd never looked at so many cars in her life, but not one of them was a white Corvette. Maybe Toby was right. Maybe the car was hundreds of miles away. . . .

"Val! I found it!"

Val sat up, her tiredness suddenly forgotten. Toby skidded to a stop beside her and leaped off his bike. His face was flushed, and he was grinning so broadly it seemed his face would split in two.

"You're kidding! Where is it?" she cried, scrambling to her feet.

"I'll show you. Come on — it's not more than two blocks away!"

Val leaped onto her bike. "You really found it? Honest and truly?"

"No joke. Follow me. It's sitting in the driveway of a big white house on Eastview Place," Toby shouted.

Together they biked down winding, tree-lined

streets. Toby pulled up in front of a big white Colonial-style mansion and Val stopped beside him. Her heart seemed to skip a beat — or maybe several.

"Toby, that's Lila's house!" she gasped. Her voice was a whisper.

She'd only been to Lila's house once, when the Bascombes had invited all of Lila's classmates to her twelfth birthday party a year ago. But this was the house, all right.

"Well, what do you know!" Toby said. "What do we do now?"

"You're absolutely sure that's the car?" Val asked, staring at the white Corvette.

"Of course I'm sure! I'd know that car anywhere. I thought the license plate said CLOUD, but it says CLOUT. It's the right one, no doubt about it. Who do you think it belongs to? Lila's dad?"

Val shook her head. "I've seen Mr. Bascombe drop Lila off at school in a big *red* car. I bet it belongs to Lila's sister, Lauren. She graduated from high school last June, and I remember Lila saying that her folks had bought Lauren a sports car as a graduation present. Lauren goes to Gettysburg College now, but she lives at home since Gettysburg is only about half an hour away. It must have been Lauren who hit Rex!"

Suddenly everything was a lot more complicated. It was one thing to chase after a faceless person. It was very different when that person had a face and a name, a face and a name you knew. Though Val didn't know Lauren very well, she'd always admired her. Lauren wasn't nasty, like Lila. Everybody liked Lauren. Val just couldn't picture her speeding, hitting an animal, then running away. When Lauren was in high school, she'd even helped out at the Humane Society's animal shelter.

"Val Taylor! What are *you* doing here?"

Val looked up guiltily. Lila had just come out of the house and was standing on the veranda, glaring at Val. Then she saw Toby, and smiled. "And Toby! What a nice surprise!"

"I . . . uh . . . we were just riding by . . ." Val mumbled.

"That's right," Toby said, a friendly grin on his face. "We were riding by, and I saw this great car, so I made Val stop so I could take a closer look."

"Uh . . . yes, that's right," Val said.

"It sure is neat," Toby continued.

Lila came down the steps. "It is, isn't it? It belongs to my sister, Lauren. My parents gave it to her when she graduated from Franklin High last June. When I graduate, they're going to give me one, too. The minute I turn sixteen, I'm going to get my driver's license."

"Well, I guess we ought to be moving along,"

Val suggested. But Toby didn't seem to hear her. He walked over to the car and stroked a fender as though it were a favorite pet.

"How fast can this thing go?" he asked.

"Probably more than a hundred miles an hour, I bet," Lila said. "But Lauren never drives very fast. She treats that car like it was made of glass. Lauren's very cautious — like my mother. I'm the adventurous one in the family." She fluttered her eyelashes at Toby. "I bet you're that way, too."

"Yeah, I guess I am," Toby said. He still wore that idiotic grin.

Val was beginning to get annoyed.

"If I had a car like this," Toby was saying, "I'd want to see what it could do. I'd take it out on the York Road, maybe, and see how fast it could go."

Lila's face lit up. "Oh, I know exactly what you mean. But Lauren wouldn't. Like I said, she's really cautious. She'd be afraid of having an accident or something."

"Toby, we have to start back," Val said sharply. "It's getting late."

"Yeah, okay. Well, Lila, nice running into you again."

He and Val got back on their bikes and started off, leaving Lila standing by the car.

"Honestly, Toby, I thought you'd never stop

gabbing," Val said irritably as they rode off side by side.

"How else was I supposed to find out vital information?" Toby asked.

"What vital information? What are you talking about?"

Toby sighed. "You weren't paying attention. Some detective you are! I learned a lot of stuff, and you would have, too, if you hadn't been so uptight about her catching us in her driveway."

"You're right. I *was* uptight," Val admitted. "I felt like some kind of spy or something!"

"That's exactly what we were doing — spying!" Toby said excitedly. "But a good spy doesn't get all bent out of shape when someone catches him at it. So I just played it cool and let Lila talk. . . . Hey, want some ice cream?"

Toby's sudden change of subject caught Val by surprise. "Uh . . . yes, I guess."

"Come on. There's a Curran's Ice Cream Parlor on the corner of Princess and King. My treat, okay?"

"Sure. Why not?" said Val. She was hot and tired, and the idea of ice cream was irresistible, especially Curran's ice cream. It was the very best. As she pedaled along beside Toby, she said, "Are you ever going to tell me what this 'vital information' is?"

"After we get the ice cream," Toby told her with an infuriating grin.

Chapter 4

A little while later, Val and Toby were sitting at a table in Curran's Ice Cream Parlor. Val had ordered a double scoop of black raspberry, her favorite. Toby was digging into a butterscotch-marshmallow sundae with strawberry ice cream, sprinkled with chocolate chips and lots of peanuts, and topped with whipped cream and a cherry.

"So what did we learn?" Val asked.

"First, we definitely established that the car belongs to Lila's sister," Toby said through a mouthful of sundae.

"That's what I *told* you," said Val. "Big deal."

"Val, you're just not thinking like a detective — or a spy, whatever," Toby explained patiently. "You told me you *thought* the car belonged to Lauren. Now we *know* it does."

"So?"

"So now we know it's Lauren's car."

"Right. And that means it had to be Lauren who hit Rex."

42

"Wrong!" Toby's eyes were gleaming with excitement. "Remember what Lila said about Lauren never, ever speeding? Well, when I saw that car, it was speeding, all right. So if Lila's telling the truth, it wasn't Lauren who was driving."

"But who else could it have been?" Val asked.

"That's the interesting part, the *vital* part. I think somebody *stole* the car and took it for a joyride, and the person who stole it hit Rex! Now there's a case for the police!"

"Hey, you're right!" Val cried. "If we could prove that the car was stolen, they'd sit up and take notice." She dipped into her black raspberry. "But how *do* we prove it? And if it had been stolen, wouldn't Lila have mentioned it? And why would the thief have returned the car?"

"Maybe the cops caught the thief red-handed," said Toby eagerly. "Maybe the guy's in jail right now, and the police returned the car. Or maybe they found the car, but the thief's still on the loose! We might be able to catch the thief and get some kind of reward!"

Val looked at him skeptically. "Toby, you're dreaming! We don't want a reward. All we want is to find out who hit Rex." She thought a minute. "It wouldn't be a bad idea to find out if there's a car thief in the jail, though. But how do we do that?"

"No problem," Toby said cheerfully. "My dad

knows the chief of police real well. They go bowling every Friday night. I'll ask him to call Chief Ferguson and ask. And then I'll call you and tell you what he says."

He looked at his empty dish. "I could really go for another one of these, but I guess we'd better be getting home. Wonder what my mom's making for dinner? I'm starved!"

Val couldn't wait to tell Doc about finding the car. As she hopped off her bike in the driveway, she saw his car. Good! He was home early for once. Maybe he had good news for her, too. It would be so wonderful if Rex's leg was better!

"Dad, guess what! Toby and I found the white Corvette! And you'll never guess who it belongs to, never in a million years!" Val cried as she burst in the door.

"Good for you, honey," Doc said. But his smile was a little strained. Before she could ask what was wrong, Teddy came down the stairs with Frank draped around his neck. His face was solemn.

"Dad had to cut the collie's leg off," he said. "He didn't want to, but it was all infected so he had to do it."

Val's excitement faded abruptly. Tears stung her eyes. "Oh, no! Poor Rex!"

Doc rubbed his beard, the way he always did

when he was upset. "I'm sorry, Vallie. I even had Dr. Callahan come and take a look at it, and he agreed that the leg had to come off. I'm going back to Animal Inn tonight after supper to check on Rex — want to come?"

Val nodded. "Oh, yes, please! I guess nobody came to claim him, did they?"

"Afraid not," Doc said. "Either his owner hasn't seen the signs you and Toby put up, or perhaps he was dumped by someone who was just passing through town."

"Daddy, do people really *do* that?" asked Erin. She had just come into the living room, still wearing the leotard and tights she'd worn to ballet class that afternoon.

"I'm afraid they do, Erin," Doc said. "Sometimes people move from a big house into an apartment where there isn't room for a pet, or they just get tired of taking care of it. Instead of taking the animal to a shelter or trying to find it a good home, they abandon it. Maybe that's what happened with Rex."

"That stinks!" Teddy said. "But that's not what Eric did with old Frank here. He gave him to me because he knew we'd give him a good home. And we will, Dad, won't we?"

"I told you, Teddy, I have to think about it. Remember, we have four hamsters, four rabbits, two dogs, one cat, one canary, and one duck. That's enough pets for three families."

"And one horse," Erin reminded him. "You forgot about The Ghost."

"Whose side are you on, anyway?" Teddy said, glaring at his sister.

"Dad . . ." said Val, "if nobody *does* come for Rex, how would you feel about having three dogs?"

Doc groaned. "I was wondering how long it would take you to come up with that idea!"

Mrs. Racer had heard the conversation and now she said, "Doc, I have an idea about that collie. The Gebharts have a big collie dog. Their farm's right next to m'son Henry's place. He was telling me last night that they've been away for the past week visiting Mrs. Gebhart's folks. Their hired man's been so busy, taking care of the farm and all, that he didn't have time to look for him. If the collie ran off, I don't guess he'd have seen those signs Vallie and Toby put up. The Gebharts are supposed to be coming back tomorrow. I'll ask m'son Henry to find out if their dog's missing." She shook her head sadly. "M'son Henry says little Amos sets great store by that dog. He'd sure be sad if anything happened to it."

"Oh, Mrs. Racer," Val cried, "do you know Mr. Gebhart's first name? I could look him up in the phone book and call him."

"No I don't," said Mrs. Racer. "And if I did, it

wouldn't do any good. They're Amish, and the Amish don't hold with things like telephones.''

"No telephones?" said Toby, his eyes as round as saucers. "I knew the Amish didn't drive cars, but they don't have telephones either?"

"Gosh!" Erin said. "They're even more old-fashioned than the Mennonites!"

"That's right," said Mrs. Racer with a smile. Then she glanced over at the ferret, which was still wrapped around Teddy's neck, and her smile faded. "Teddy Taylor, don't you dare let that weasel into my kitchen again! It sneaked out of your room today and stole some of the cookies I was baking for the dance at Vallie's school. Ate 'em quick as a wink, it did!"

"I'm sorry, Mrs. Racer," Teddy said, hanging his head. "I guess maybe that's because I've been telling him that you make the best cookies in the whole world, and he decided to find out for himself."

Mrs. Racer's stern expression softened just a bit. "Well, maybe. But I don't want that thieving weasel stealing my cookies, no matter how good they are!"

Later that evening, Val was kneeling by Rex's pen in Animal Inn's intensive care unit, stroking the collie's silky golden head. The dog's eyes were cloudy and his nose felt hot. Val tried not to look at the bandaged stump, or at the tubes that were keeping

47

fluids and nutrients flowing into his body. The collie's tail wagged weakly in response to her touch.

"Dad, he's not in very good shape, is he?" she whispered.

"I'm afraid not, Vallie," Doc said. "He's not responding to treatment as I hoped he would. The operation took a lot out of him."

"Is he going to die?" Val asked softly.

"I don't know. I honestly don't know. We're doing everything we can. Only time will tell." Doc touched her shoulder. "Have you said hello to The Ghost? I think he misses you."

"He sure does," said Mike, who had been tending to the other animals. "He asked me this afternoon, 'Where's Vallie? Haven't seen her in a couple of days. Think she's forgotten all about me, Mike?' And I said to him, 'The day Vallie forgets about you will be the day pigs fly!' That's what I told him. Seemed to cheer him up a whole lot."

Val forced a smile. She knew that Mike was just trying to cheer *her* up. Mike was the only person she knew who talked to animals as though they were people, just the way she did. But to hear Mike tell it, the animals actually talked back!

"I miss him a whole lot," she said. "I think I'll go say hi to him now. There's nothing I can do for Rex. . . . I'll only be a minute."

The Ghost whickered softly as Val entered his stall in the Large Animal Clinic. She put her arms around his neck and rested her cheek against him.

"I'm sorry I've neglected you," she told him. "And I haven't forgotten about you. I could never forget about you! But I've had so many things on my mind. Rex isn't getting any better. I'm afraid he's going to die! Oh, Ghost, it makes me so sad when animals get hurt! I want so much to help them, but I can't. Sometimes even Doc can't."

Val stood like that for a long time.

"Vallie? Time to go home, honey." Doc's voice came out of the shadows beyond the door of The Ghost's stall.

Val nodded and sniffled.

"Here — blow," Doc said, offering the big bright bandanna he always carried in his hip pocket.

Val blew and wiped her eyes. "Maybe I'll never be a good vet," she said as they left the barn. "Not if I can't help crying every time an animal doesn't get better right away."

Doc put his arm around her shoulders. "You're going to be a fine vet," he assured her. "Caring is the most important thing, and you care so much. You just can't let your emotions run away with you, that's all."

"I know. But sometimes it isn't easy," Val sighed.

49

"No, it isn't," Doc agreed. "Sometimes it's very hard indeed."

* * *

When they got back to the house, Erin told Val that Toby had phoned and left a weird message. " 'No car thieves,' he said. What was he talking about?" she asked.

"Oh, just some crazy idea he had," Val answered. She didn't feel like going into the whole story right now. It *had* been a crazy idea, all right, but Toby had been so excited about it that he'd convinced her that it just might be possible. Now they were right back at square one — or maybe square two, since at least they'd discovered who the car belonged to. But what good did that do? And where did they go from there? The only thing Val could think of to do was to tackle Lila and tell her straight out that she knew it was Lauren's car that had injured the dog. What would Lila have to say to that? Nothing very nice, Val was sure. But what else could she do?

She could talk to Doc.

After Mrs. Racer had left, Teddy (and Frank) had been put to bed, and Erin had reluctantly taken off her leotard and tights and gone to her room, Val found her father in the den, reading. Jocko and Sunshine were stretched out on the rug by his feet. He looked up when he saw Val.

"What's up, Vallie?" he asked.

Val came in and sat down on the hassock next to his leather armchair. "Dad, like I told you, Toby and I found the car today."

"So you did. But things got kind of confused, so I never had a chance to find out where and how. Want to tell me now?"

"It belongs to Lila Bascombe's sister!"

"Well, that's a surprise, all right," Doc said thoughtfully as he put down his magazine. "How did you discover it?"

Val filled him in with the details, including Toby's suggestion that the car might have been stolen, and the fact that it hadn't been.

"So it had to be Lauren, Dad. She must have hit Rex and didn't say anything to anybody."

Doc frowned. "That doesn't sound like Lauren Bascombe. She's not the kind of girl to behave in such a reckless manner. Isn't it possible that she loaned the car to somebody, or that somebody borrowed it without her knowledge?"

"I guess so," Val said. "What should I do now, Dad?"

Doc thought for a while. At last he said, "The only thing you can do is tell Lila that Toby is sure that her sister's car hit Rex, and see how she reacts. But you have to consider the fact that Lila may know nothing about it. And even if she does, there's no guarantee that she'll care enough to do anything about it."

"That's the whole problem." Val sighed. "Lila doesn't care about anything except Lila!"

"I think you must mention it to her," said Doc. "At least it will make the Bascombes realize that somebody, whether it was Lauren or somebody else, was driving irresponsibly and endangered a life. And if that doesn't get any results, I'll talk to George Bascombe myself. Okay?"

Val leaned her head against her father's knee. "Okay. But I ought to be able to handle it myself — or at least, I hope so."

Cleveland stalked into the study and rubbed against Val's leg. Then he went over to Sunshine, the big golden retriever, and curled up next to the dog. Cleveland and Sunshine were best friends. If Jocko were awake, he'd have chased Cleveland right out of the room. But he wasn't, so the three animals lay peacefully together.

Val thought about Amos, the little Amish boy. Suppose Rex really was his dog? He'd come home from his trip and there would be no big friendly collie to welcome him. But if he found out where Rex was, he'd find him again, and he'd be so happy! Wouldn't it be wonderful if Rex had a family at last? Maybe he'd start getting better right away!

52

Chapter 5

Val had worried about how to approach Lila, but the next morning in art class as Val was concentrating on her ceramics project, Lila came over and sat down next to her.

"That's a nice dog you're making, Val," Lila said with a big, bright smile. "It's a collie, isn't it? I could tell by the long pointy nose. I'm making a jewelry box, see? I was going to give it to my mother, but now I think I'll keep it for myself. I'm going to glaze it pink. Pink's my favorite color." Lila moved closer to Val. "How's your friend Toby? He's really cute. You ought to invite him to the Harvest Dance. Funny — he's not the kind of boy I'd have pictured hanging out with you. . . ." She giggled. "That sounds awful! What I meant was, you've never seemed interested in boys, and none of the boys in school are interested in you. Did Toby ask you about me?"

Val said, "Actually he talked mostly about Lauren's car."

"I could tell he was impressed," Lila said smugly. "What did he say exactly?"

Val sculpted some lines in the collie's coat to represent fur. Avoiding Lila's eyes, she said, "He told me that he thought it was the car he'd seen speeding on the York Road on Tuesday, the one that hit a dog that was running across the street." She glanced up and saw Lila's super-friendly smile disappear.

"Oh, he did, did he?" Lila said sharply. "Why didn't he tell me that yesterday?"

"I guess it just struck him later, when we were having our ice cream," Val mumbled.

"Well, he's wrong! It had to be another car. Lauren would never do anything like that. Like I told you, she's a really cautious driver. . . ." Lila's eyes suddenly widened. "Did you say Tuesday?"

Val nodded. "And the dog was very badly hurt. My dad had to amputate one of its legs. We still don't know if Rex will get better."

Lila shrugged. "Oh, who cares about some old dog! I don't know who hit him, but if it happened on Tuesday, it couldn't possibly have been Lauren who was driving." She stopped abruptly.

"*I* care about 'some old dog'!" Val said angrily, not even noticing how suddenly Lila had stopped talking. "How can you be so sure it wasn't Lauren? Toby's positive it was her car. He remembered the license plate. Lila, that dog just might *die*! Maybe he's just a dumb animal to you, but animals have rights, too. Will you talk to Lauren, ask her if she hit a big, beautiful collie? Because if she did, she ought to know that dog is in very bad shape, and she shouldn't be so reckless."

Lila poked at the sections of her jewelry box, scowling. "I will not! And don't get any ideas about talking to her yourself. If you do, I'll tell her that it's all a pack of lies. Your hick farmer friend Toby Curran must be blind or something — just like that dumb old horse of yours!"

Mr. Haines, the art teacher, looked over at their table. "Lila, please keep your voice down. Other people are trying to work."

Gathering up the pieces of her box, Lila hissed in Val's ear, "Don't you dare speak to Lauren! If you do, you'll be sorry. *Real* sorry!" She reached out and pressed her thumb down into the middle of the clay collie's back. The little figure collapsed.

Val stared at her, boiling inside yet unable to say a word. Lila marched over to another table and sat down. Her face was strained and pale.

Val looked down at her clay sculpture. One of its legs was completely crushed. Furious, she blinked back scalding tears as she began to repair it.

". . . And then she deliberately smashed my dog! It was like she couldn't stand to have anybody say anything against Lauren," Val said to Jill at lunch that day in the cafeteria. "She said I'd be sorry if I said anything to Lauren, and she meant it." She stirred her yogurt viciously with a plastic spoon. "I was so mad, I could have killed her!"

"That's weird," Jill said thoughtfully. "I mean, I never thought Lila was so fond of Lauren that she'd get all upset over something like this."

"She was upset, all right," Val said. "She went absolutely white. I guess it's like Mrs. Racer always says — blood is thicker than water, even Lila's blood."

Jill shook her head. "I'm sorry, I just don't buy it. I've heard Lila talk about her sister, and she's never had one good word to say about Lauren. So why should she get all bent out of shape because Lauren might be in trouble? Knowing Lila, I can't help thinking there's something fishy going on."

"Now you sound like Toby," Val sighed. "He always makes things out to be much more complicated than they really are. I guess we just have to accept that Lila really loves her sister deep down, and she can't stand to have anyone say anything bad about her. I know I'd feel the same way if somebody told me Teddy or Erin had done something awful. I'd probably blow up just the way Lila did."

"Maybe. But you wouldn't smash her ceramics project just because you were mad," Jill said. "That was just plain Lila-mean!"

"No, I probably wouldn't," Val agreed. "But if Lila hadn't gone to the other table when she did, I just might have turned her precious jewelry box back into a ball of clay!"

"I wish you had!" Jill said. She looked at her watch. "Gosh, I have to run. I have to check with Miss Becker about some stuff for the dance. Speaking of the dance, why don't you ask Toby to come?"

"Funny," said Val. "Lila made the same suggestion."

Jill made a face. "Yuck! I hate to agree with that girl about anything! See you in bio, okay?"

"Okay. See you."

Jill hurried off with her tray, leaving Val to finish her yogurt and veggiburger. She and Jill had chosen a small table near the windows of the cafeteria rather than sitting with their friends as they usually did. As she munched her bean sprouts, Val wondered what she should do now. Should she go to Lauren in spite of Lila's threat? But what if Toby really *had* made a mistake? What if there was another white Corvette, one with the license plate CLOUD as he'd first thought? She didn't want to accuse anyone unjustly.

"What's up, Lila?"

Over the cheerful din in the cafeteria, Val heard a boy's voice. She was pretty sure it was Jeff Willard. She hadn't noticed him and Lila coming over to the table behind her. She hoped Lila wouldn't see her sitting there, her back to them.

"Plenty!" she heard Lila say. "Why didn't you tell me. . . ." Lila's voice sank into a whisper, and Val couldn't hear the rest. She knew eavesdropping was wrong, but she couldn't help straining her ears to catch what Lila and Jeff were saying.

"So what's the big deal?" Jeff asked. "Some dog got run over. It wasn't my fault. Dogs get hit by cars all the time. Their owners ought to keep them tied up. I didn't tell you because. . . ." Again Val couldn't hear. She was puzzled. Had Jeff seen the accident, too, like Toby? Then she heard her name.

"Val Taylor's the big deal," Lila said. "She's an animal nut, and she's real mad because her hick friend said he saw Lauren's car hit that dog. She's asking a lot of questions, and if she talks to Lauren, there's going to be big trouble."

Val was getting more confused by the minute. She was also getting pretty tired of hearing Lila call Toby names. She'd changed her tune, all right, since she'd first met him! Val had finished her lunch. She knew she ought to pick up her tray and leave, but she couldn't. It was as if she were glued to her chair.

"Hey, Lila, take it easy. It wasn't my fault," Jeff said. "It wasn't like I was driving or anything."

"Jeff, I know that. I'm not blaming you. I'm just saying you should have told me, that's all," Lila whined. "If my folks find out, I don't know what they'll do!"

What was Lila so afraid of her parents' finding out? Jill was right. There was something fishy going on. But what?

The bell sounded for the end of the lunch period. Val waited for Lila and Jeff to leave, then picked up her tray and headed for the door. If Toby were here, playing Sherlock Holmes, he'd probably say she'd just received a lot more valuable information. And maybe she had, but she didn't like to think where that information was leading. It sounded very much as though Lauren *had* been driving the car in spite of what Lila had said in art class that morning. Val just couldn't picture Lauren doing anything like that.

When she got to Animal Inn after school, Val decided she'd tell Toby everything. Maybe he could come up with an explanation.

And maybe, just maybe, the Gebharts would turn up and say that Rex was their dog. Rex would get better then, Val was sure. She'd read that animals who were really sick or badly injured could sometimes get better if the people they loved were there to take care of them. Even the best vet couldn't help an animal that didn't have the will to live.

Val loved Rex, but he didn't know her very well. He couldn't know how much she and Doc wanted him to recover, though she'd told him again and again. And every time she talked to Rex, he wagged his tail. But it wasn't the same thing as having your very own person patting you and telling you how much he cared.

"Hey, Val, wait up!" Her friend Sarah Jones caught up to her. "I saw the flier you put up about the collie. Find his owner yet?"

"No, not yet. But we're hoping somebody will show up at Animal Inn today," Val said.

"I guess you haven't found out who hit him, have you?" Sarah asked.

"Well, not exactly." Remembering that she was supposed to be a detective, Val added, "We have a lot of clues, but we haven't found the driver."

"When you do, I hope you throw the book at him — or her!" Sarah said.

Val sighed. "I wish we could. It's not going to be easy, though."

No, it certainly wasn't going to be easy, she thought as she and Sarah walked side-by-side down the hall to the bio lab. In fact, it was getting more complicated by the minute.

"I can't believe somebody would bring a dog to Animal Inn just to get his toenails cut," Toby said later that afternoon. He and Val were holding down a large, unhappy black Labrador retriever while Doc trimmed the dog's overgrown nails.

Doc said, "Dogs that don't get regular exercise on pavements often develop 'Dragon Lady' toenails, Toby. The pavement wears down their nails, kind of like a file would. Their owners are scared to cut them because they're afraid that they'll hit one of the little veins there. Light-colored dogs have light-colored nails so you can see where the blood vessels end. Dark dogs, like Nicky here, present a problem."

Nicky moaned, struggled, and would have escaped if Val had not grabbed him firmly and whispered soothing words into one black ear.

"Only four more to go, Nicky,"she promised. The big black dog whined. "Nicky's a terrible coward," she told Toby. "The minute he sees the clippers, he goes bananas. It doesn't hurt him, anymore than it hurts you to cut your fingernails. Only Nicky doesn't remember from one time to the next. He isn't very bright, but he's a nice dog, anyway."

"Vallie's never met an animal she didn't like," Doc said, smiling at Val. He gave one last snip to Nicky's nails. "Okay, that does it, fella."

Nicky wagged his tail, and wiggled all over with joy and relief.

"Hand me that syringe, Vallie," Doc added. "Nicky's also due for his rabies shot. Compared to the agony he just went through having his toenails cut, this will be a cinch."

And it was. The dog didn't even seem to notice

61

the injection, and Toby took him out to his owner in the waiting room.

"Dad, how's Rex doing? I didn't have time to check on him when I came in," said Val.

Doc's smile faded. He turned away to wash up. Instead of answering her question, he said, "Vallie, hand me a towel, will you?"

Val did. "Dad, he's worse, isn't he?" she asked softly.

"Vallie. . . ." Doc met her eyes, and right then she knew.

"He's dead. Rex is dead! Oh, Dad, why didn't you tell me?" Val cried.

"There wasn't time," Doc said wearily. "It's been a madhouse around here today. Rex began bleeding internally. I couldn't save him. I'm sorry, Vallie. I did my best."

Toby struck his head into the treatment room. "You ready for the next patient, Doc?" he asked. He saw Val's face, and looked from her to Doc. "What's the matter? Something wrong?"

"Rex died this afternoon," Doc told him. "Ask Mr. Stauffer and Snoopy to wait a few minutes, please. I'll be right with them."

Toby's face fell. "Gee, that's terrible! He was such a neat dog. . . . Should I tell Mr. Stauffer to bring Snoopy back tomorrow?"

Doc shook his head. "No. Snoopy has a badly

infected ear. I'll take care of it. But first I have to talk to Vallie."

"Whatever you say," said Toby, and closed the door.

Val was standing by the sink, tearing the paper towel Doc had used into tiny strips. Tears streamed down her cheeks. She tried not to sob out loud, but it felt like there was a huge rock in her throat — kind of like when she ate a hard-boiled egg too fast and could hardly breathe.

Doc put his arm around her and kissed the top of her head. "I know how you feel, Vallie. Toby's right. Rex *was* a neat dog. I wish I could have saved his life, but it wasn't possible. He was too badly injured. Do you understand, Vallie?"

Val brushed away the tears with the sleeve of her lab coat. "I — I understand. I hate it, but I understand." She threw her arms around her father. "And I know you hate it, too!"

Doc held her close. "Yes, Vallie, I really do hate it. I wish I could make every animal well, but sometimes that just isn't possible. And life goes on, honey. Right now there's a poor miserable dog out there that needs to be taken care of. I'll need your help, Vallie. Snoopy Stauffer doesn't like having his ear tended to any more than Nicky liked having his toenails cut."

Val wiped her eyes with what was left of the paper towel. "I'll help you, Dad. You know I will.

But . . . what's going to happen to Rex?"

"If no one shows up to claim him, we'll have to cremate him," Doc said.

Val nodded miserably.

Toby stuck his head in again. "Doc, I'm sorry to interrupt, but there's somebody here about Rex. I didn't know what to tell them."

"I'll talk to them, Toby," Doc said. "Ask them to take a seat. I'll be right there."

"Who is it?" Val asked.

"I don't know their names, but they're Amish. They parked their buggy next to Doc's car," Toby told her. "It's a man and his son. The kid looks to be about six or seven, I guess."

Val looked up at Doc. "It must be the people Mrs. Racer told us about. Little Amos Gebhart and his father. Oh, Dad, how can we tell them?"

"I'll handle it, Vallie," Doc said gently.

"I'll go with you," said Val. "Maybe I won't be able to do any good, but I have to be there."

Doc touched her shoulder, his face solemn. "Think you can talk to them without breaking down?"

Val nodded. "I think I can. I hope I can. Amos has to know that his dog got the best possible care by people who loved him a lot. And I did! I loved Rex a lot."

"I know, Vallie. So did I. It might help Amos to know how much we care."

Hand in hand, father and daughter went out into the waiting room. Val saw Mr. Stauffer, with Snoopy sitting patiently by his side — and a bearded man in a broad-brimmed black hat, black pants and vest, and a bright blue shirt. The man's hair was long, and he didn't have a moustache, only a beard. Beside him on one of Animal Inn's benches sat a little boy dressed exactly like his father. Eager blue eyes peered out from behind steel-rimmed spectacles.

"Mr. Gebhart?" Doc asked, going over to the man and extending his hand.

"That's right," the man said.

"I'm Doctor Taylor," Doc said. "This is my daughter, Valentine. We've been caring for the collie that was hit by a car on Wednesday."

"Might be Luke," Mr. Gebhart said. "We've been away. Our hired man told me Luke slipped his collar the other day — hasn't seen him since. Sounds like it might be our dog. How's he doing?"

"Is he going to be all right?" the little boy asked. "Luke's almost as old as me — I'm seven. We can take him home if he's all better. Luke's my best friend."

"Mr. Gebhart, I think you'd better come with me," Doc said. "You can tell me if it's your dog."

"Can I come, too?" the boy asked.

"You'd better wait here," Doc told him. "It will only take a minute."

He and Mr. Gebhart left the waiting room. Val felt miserable. If it *was* the Gebharts' dog, Amos was in for an awful shock.

Mr. Stauffer, who had been waiting patiently for Doc to treat Snoopy's ear, spoke up. "You like dogs, young man?"

Amos nodded. "Sure. I have a collie. His name's Luke. What's your dog's name?"

"Snoopy. He's a bassett hound. You like bassett hounds?"

Amos considered Snoopy carefully. "He's kind of droopy-looking."

"All bassett hounds are droopy-looking!" Mr. Stauffer reached down to pet his dog. "Snoopy's ear's infected. Doc says it might be a tumor. But Doc Taylor's a real good vet. He'll fix him up. Your dog sick?"

"He ain't sick. A car hit him. Only it might not be him. My pop's gone to see," said Amos.

"Oh." Mr. Stauffer patted Snoopy. "If it's him, I hope he's okay."

"Me, too," said Amos.

"I have two dogs," Val said quickly. "And a cat, four hamsters, a duck, and some rabbits. And my sister has a canary, and my brother has a ferret."

"What's a ferret?" Amos asked.

"It's like a weasel, only nicer . . . Val began. But before she could go on, Doc and Mr. Gebhart came back. She looked up, and Doc nodded. Her heart sank.

Doc went over to Amos and sat down beside the little boy.

"Is it Luke?" Amos asked.

"Your father says it is. Amos, Luke had a really bad accident. We hoped we could make him better, but it didn't work out that way." Doc paused, then went on. "It was such a bad accident that he couldn't get well. We took real good care of him, but . . . Amos, Luke died today. I'm sorry. We did everything we could."

"He died? Luke's *dead*?" Amos whispered, staring at Doc.

Val kneeled down in front of him. "We loved him a lot, Amos. Not as much as you loved him, I guess, but we really did love him. If anyone could have saved his life, Dad would have. We're . . . awfully sorry."

Amos just looked at her. He didn't say a word, but two fat tears slid down his cheeks.

"It wasn't your fault," Mr. Gebhart said gruffly. "It wasn't anybody's fault except whoever hit him. Too bad. Luke was a good dog."

Amos got up then and went over to his father. Mr. Gebhart put an arm around the boy's shoulders.

"What would you like us to do with him?" Doc asked.

"Guess we'd better take him home," said Mr. Gebhart. He looked down at Amos. "We'll bury him under the pear tree out back, all right? It's real pretty in the spring when all the blossoms are out."

Amos nodded. His face was so sad that Val wanted to cry. But she didn't. Amos was being so brave that she would have been ashamed.

Toby had been standing by, ready to do anything that might be helpful. Now Doc turned to him.

"Toby, bring Rex — *Luke* — out and put him in Mr. Gebhart's buggy, please."

"I'll do it," said Mr. Gehbart. "I'll carry him out myself." He shook hands with Doc again. "Thanks for all you done, Doctor. How much do I owe you for taking care of Luke?"

"Nothing," Doc said. "As Vallie told you, we were very fond of your dog. You don't owe me anything, Mr. Gebhart."

The man frowned. "We don't take charity. What do I owe you?"

Doc hesitated, then said, "All right. How about a couple of chickens, and some vegetables? That would cover it."

Mr. Gebhart thought about it. Finally he nodded. "Six chickens, two dozen eggs, vegetables, and half a hog when we butcher next month."

Val winced, but managed a smile. "That sounds real good, Mr. Gebhart," she said, and Doc agreed.

Mr. Gebhart and Amos followed Toby out of the waiting room. A few minutes later, they returned. Mr. Gebhart was carrying the collie, Amos trotting at his side. The lump in Val's throat was so big she thought she might suffocate when she saw the big golden dog lying there so still. She held the door open so Mr. Gebhart and Amos could go outside. Then she, Doc, and Toby went out, too.

The Gebhart's black buggy looked strange next to Doc's car and the Animal Inn van. A glossy bay horse stood between the shafts.

Mr. Gebhart gently lifted the dog into the back of the buggy. Amos untied the horse, then climbed up onto the front seat beside his father.

"Chickens, eggs, vegetables, and half a hog," Mr. Gebhart repeated, flicking the reins over the bay's smooth back.

"Good-bye, Rex," Val whispered as the buggy rolled off down Orchard Lane.

"Luke," Toby corrected. His voice sounded funny, like he wanted to cry, too, but wouldn't let himself — just like Val.

"Luke," said Val. "Good-bye, Luke. I'm glad you're going home at last."

She hadn't had a chance to tell Toby about the conversation she'd overheard between Lila and Jeff earlier. But she'd tell him now, and they'd find out who was responsible for the collie's death.

69

Chapter
6

Because he knew how upset both Val and Toby were about the collie's death, Doc asked Toby to have supper at the Taylors' that night. After Toby called his mother to ask her permission, Val called Mrs. Racer to tell her Toby was coming. There would be plenty of food, Val knew. Mrs. Racer always cooked enough for a small army.

Val couldn't wait to talk to Toby about what she's heard Lila and Jeff talking about. But when they came into the house, Erin met them at the door. She looked furious!

"Daddy," she said to Doc, "You have to do something about that ferret! He almost killed Dandelion today!" Dandelion, usually called Dandy, was Erin's canary.

"Calm down, honey," Doc said, kissing her flushed cheek. "What happened? And where's Teddy?"

"He's in his room," Erin told him. "Mrs. Racer sent him there afterward."

"After what?" Doc asked patiently. "Start at the beginning."

"Well, Frank got loose again this afternoon, and Jocko started chasing him. He chased him right up the stairs and into *my* room! And Frank ran under my bed, and Jocko followed him, and then Frank went under the bureau, and Jocko went after him, and he knocked down the stand of Dandy's cage, and I thought Dandy was going to have a *heart attack*, I really did, Daddy! He was fluttering and squawking something terrible! He might have broken his wings! And it's all that awful ferret's fault."

"That was *after* I found that weasel in my kitchen again, stealing the food from Jocko's dish," Mrs. Racer said, bustling into the living room. "And *after* Teddy had given him a whole popsicle to eat! He couldn't have been hungry. Weasels are just plain mean. Doc, you got to get rid of that animal. There won't be a minute's peace in this house until you do."

Val spoke up then. "Mrs. Racer, the Gebharts came to Animal Inn today. Rex was their dog, only his real name is — *was* — Luke. He died."

Mrs. Racer and Erin both gasped.

"Oh, no!" Erin cried. "Oh, Daddy, I'm so sorry. I didn't know. That little boy must feel just terrible."

"We all do, Erin," Doc said. "Mrs. Racer, I'll speak to Teddy about the ferret. I know that having him here is hard on you — and on Dandelion. We'll have to find him another home."

"I know the perfect place," Toby put in. "There are these people who have started a ferret farm near our place."

"Are they the people in that *Gazette* article?" Val asked.

"That's them. Jack and Terry Detwiler. I bet they'd love to take Frank," said Toby. "Want me to ask them?"

"That just might be an excellent solution," Doc said. "I think I'd better go up and talk to Teddy."

After Doc had gone upstairs, Erin had trotted down to the basement to practice some new ballet steps, Mrs. Racer had been picked up by her son Henry, and Val and Toby had settled down in the living room. Val was sitting on the sofa, Cleveland in her lap, and Toby was sprawled in front of the fireplace, Jocko on one side of him, and Sunshine on the other.

"I talked to Lila today," Val said, stroking Cleveland's thick orange fur.

"What did she say?" Toby asked.

"She said Lauren couldn't possibly have been driving the car that hit Luke. She seemed absolutely positive, and it had something to do with its being Tuesday."

"Tuesday? What's so special about Tuesday?"

"Search me," Val said. "All I can tell you is she got really uptight when I told her Rex — Luke — had been hit on Tuesday. She hollered at me, and said if I said anything to Lauren, I'd be sorry. And then at lunch, I heard her talking to Jeff Willard. It was all so *peculiar*! She said he should have told her, and he said it wasn't his fault, he wasn't driving. And then she said he should have told her anyway, only I don't know what he was supposed to have told her. Then the bell rang, and I didn't hear any more. What do you think it means, Toby?"

Toby scratched Sunshine's ears, frowning. "Well, I think it means that Jeff Willard might have been *in* the car when it hit the dog, but unless he was lying, he wasn't driving."

"He wasn't lying," Val said. "Jeff's only fourteen. You can't get a driver's license in Pennsylvania until you're sixteen."

"Just because you don't have a license doesn't mean you don't know how to drive," Toby replied. "*I* know how to drive. My oldest brother taught me last year, and Dad lets me drive the truck from the dairy barn to the far pasture sometimes. I've been driving tractors on the farm for a few years, too. So if I wanted to, I could drive a car — only I wouldn't, not off the farm."

"Gee!" Val said, impressed. "I didn't know you knew how to drive."

"Well, I do. And maybe Jeff Willard does, too. And maybe he talked Lila into letting him take Lauren's car for a spin, and Lauren didn't know about it. That could be why Lila got all bent out of shape when you told her about Luke."

Val shook her head. "I don't think so, Toby. Remember, they didn't know I was listening. There was no reason for Jeff to lie to Lila. No, somebody else must have been driving the car."

"Then it had to be Lauren," Toby said, "and Jeff must have seen the accident, like I did. That's the only thing that makes sense. But I don't see what Tuesday has to do with anything."

Val sighed. "Neither can I. But I just can't believe that Lauren Bascombe would do a thing like that, and Dad agrees. She's not the kind of person who'd hit an animal and then drive away."

"How well do you know this Lauren?"

Val hesitated. "Not very well, really. I just remember how nice she was to me when we were both volunteering at the animal shelter last year. She wasn't stuck-up or anything. And I know she loves animals."

"People change," Toby told her. "They get a fancy car, they go to college — maybe Lauren isn't so nice anymore. It happens, Val."

"I guess," Val said, scratching Cleveland behind the ears. He purred gratefully.

She and Toby sat silently for a while, absorbed in thought. Finally Toby said, "Uh . . . Val, it was real nice of your dad to ask me for dinner. When do you usually eat? Something smells awful good."

Val couldn't help smiling. "We'll be eating in about half an hour." She stood up, and dropped Cleveland on the couch. "I better start making a salad. Want to feed the animals? I'll show you where their food is."

Mr. Curran came to pick up Toby after supper. Val tried to concentrate on her homework, but she kept seeing Amos Gebhart's sad little face, and Luke's body in Mr. Gebhart's arms as he carried the dog out of Animal Inn. She knew that it was up to her to find out who had hit Luke. Toby had been no help at all figuring out what Lila and Jeff were talking about. Nobody seemed to be very interested in Luke anymore, not even Doc. He was too busy explaining to Teddy why Frank couldn't stay at the Taylors', and Teddy was all upset about losing his new pet. Erin was worried about her canary. Dandy had been so frightened when his cage had been knocked over, she said, that he might never sing again.

Nobody cares but me, Val thought. So I'll have to do it by myself. I'll have to talk to Lauren. But how? If I call the Bascombes, Lila will know, and she'll hate me. But what do I care! What's more important — for me to find out who killed Luke, or to avoid a nasty scene with Lila? Val hated scenes. Lila could make her life miserable at Hamilton. . . .

But Luke was dead, and Amos Gebhart was an unhappy little boy. Although, Val had to admit, Amos probably wouldn't be any less unhappy if he knew who had killed his pet. The only thing that might make Amos smile would be — a new puppy!

So that's what she had to do. She had to find the person who had hit Luke and make that person give Amos another dog. Val knew it wouldn't be the same as having Luke back, but it would be better than having no dog at all.

She began to think of a plan. Lila had chorus practice after school tomorrow. Val would bike out to Wyndham Heights after school the next day and hang around until she saw Lauren return from Gettysburg in her car. Then she'd go right up to her and ask her straight out if she had hit the collie. Lauren would tell her the truth, she was sure — unless Toby was right, and Lauren had changed a lot. Val was sure she'd know if Lauren lied to her. And if that happened, if nobody would admit to being responsible for Luke's death, Val would get a puppy for Amos herself. There were lots of unwanted animals at the animal shelter. She'd adopt one for Amos, a cuddly little puppy that he'd learn to love.

"Can't I come with you?" Jill asked on Friday. Classes were over for the day and Val was mounting her bike, getting ready to carry out her plan.

"I don't think that would be a good idea," Val said. "It's bad enough that I'm going to have to try to hide behind a tree or something and wait for Lauren to come home. If there are two of us, it'll be impossible."

"I guess you're right," Jill agreed. "But I just can't believe that Lauren would do something like that. Lila, yes. But Lauren, definitely no!"

"I know what you mean," Val said. "I can't believe it, either. I have to talk to her, though. Lila will be tied up with chorus practice after school, so if Lauren comes home I'll be able to see her alone."

"What if she doesn't come home?" Jill asked. "What'll you do then?"

"Hide behind another tree tomorrow," Val said with a sigh. "Oh, Jill, I really hate all this! I wish I could think of some other way."

"Well, what else can you do? I mean, Lila isn't going to tell you anything at all. And it *is* Lauren's car. She's the only person who can tell you if she was driving it last Tuesday."

"Right." Val wheeled her bike out of the rack. "Well, here goes. I'll let you know what happens."

Jill waved as she rode off. Through the open windows of Hamilton Junior High, Val could hear the voices of the Treble Chorus (known as the "Terrible Chorus" to anyone who had ever been to one of their concerts). Lila ought to be safely occupied for the next hour at least. Now if only Lauren came home before Lila did!

As Val pedaled up Eastview Place, she looked around for a place to conceal herself until Lauren arrived. There was a big oak tree almost directly opposite the Bascombes' house. If Val left her bike in the park, she could hide behind that tree. She'd have a good view of the house, and nobody would see her there. And when Lauren drove up in her white Corvette, Val would cross the street and say. . . .

Val stared at the Bascombes' driveway. There was the white Corvette, and there was Lauren, in cut-off jeans and a T-shirt, washing her car.

Suddenly Val's courage failed her. Faced with the sight of Lauren, she didn't know what to do. She knew what she *ought* to do, but she couldn't seem to move.

I could ride around the block a couple of times, then pull up and say, "Hi, Lauren. Long time no see." And Lauren would probably say, "Who are you?" And I'd say, "You don't remember me, but I'm Valentine Taylor, and I think you killed a dog."

Val shuddered. Maybe it would be better just to go home, contact the animal shelter, and find a substitute puppy for Amos. Forget about justice! It wouldn't make any difference to Amos.

But it would make a big difference to *you*, said a little voice inside her head.

Val rode up to the driveway.

"Lauren? Hi. Can I talk to you a minute?" Her voice sounded funny, tense and strained, just the way she felt.

Lila's older sister looked up. For a moment she looked confused, then she said, "It's Val, isn't it? Val Taylor?"

Val nodded.

"If you're looking for Lila, she's still at school. The Terrible Chorus has practice this afternoon." Lauren grinned, and Val couldn't help grinning back.

"I'm not looking for Lila," she said, getting off her bike. "I was really looking for . . . you."

"Me? How come?"

Lauren dropped her sponge into the bucket of soapy water. Lauren was really beautiful, Val thought. Lila was pretty, but Lauren was so much prettier that you could only call her beautiful. And she had such a nice smile!

"I . . . I wanted to talk to you," Val said.

"Okay, talk." Lauren leaned against the car, brushing her dark bangs out of her eyes. "What's up? Lila's not in trouble, is she?"

Why did she ask that? Val wondered.

"I'm not exactly sure," Val confessed. "It's . . . your car."

"My car?" Lauren frowned. "What do you mean?"

Val took a deep breath. "Your car hit a dog on

79

the York Road on Tuesday, and yesterday the dog died. Were you driving the car then, Lauren?"

Lauren stared at her. "This past Tuesday?"

Val nodded.

"No way," Lauren said firmly. "I don't have classes on Tuesdays. I was with my mother, shopping in Philadelphia. The car was right where it is now all day — only dirtier. That's why I'm washing it. What makes you think it was my car?"

"Because my friend Toby Curran saw the accident, and he recognized it," Val said.

Lauren looked puzzled. "It couldn't have been. Unless . . . no, that's crazy. Lila *wouldn't*!"

"Wouldn't what?" Val asked.

"Lila was here after school. She'd asked her friend Jeff to come over, and I remember her saying something about Jeff's older brother Rhett being here, too. Jeff's a car freak and so is Rhett. And I left my keys on the table right inside the front door!" Lauren was getting angry now. "Lila wouldn't have let Rhett borrow my car! She knows I don't even let anyone *touch* this car — but Rhett just got his license. . . ."

"Oh no, Lauren," said Val, "I can't believe Lila would do something like that." But as soon as the words left her mouth, she knew it was exactly the kind of thing Lila *would* do in order to make points with Jeff.

"You don't know Lila the way I do," Lauren said

grimly. "She borrows everything — my perfume, my nail polish, my hair dryer, my best cashmere sweater, even the pearls Mom and Dad gave me for my sixteenth birthday! And she never even asks. But this time it's really serious!"

"But Lauren, we don't know Lila let Rhett drive your car," Val protested. "Maybe I shouldn't have said anything. . . ."

"Oh yes, you should have. It all fits too perfectly. Val, I want you to tell me exactly what happened — what time the dog was hit, what your friend saw, the whole thing. And when my little sister gets home, she's going to have a lot of questions to answer!" Lauren took a deep breath, trying to calm down, then added, "Val, listen, I'm really sorry to hear about the dog — I didn't mean to sound like the only important thing was my car. Believe me, if I had hit an animal, I'd have stopped and tried to do something to help it. I'd never just drive off and leave it there. You know that, don't you?"

"Yes," Val whispered, " I do."

Then she told Lauren everything she knew about the accident, including Doc's efforts to save Luke's life, the amputation of the dog's leg, and little Amos's sorrow and bravery when he learned his pet had died.

When she had finished, Lauren's face was grim. "You'd better go home, Val," she said. "Leave Lila to me. I'll get the truth out of her one way or another, if I have to wring her pretty little neck."

"I'm really sorry I accused you," Val said. "But everything fit, you know? Like you said, it all fit perfectly. I didn't want to believe you'd done it, but it was your car, and. . . ."

"Don't worry about it," said Lauren. "I'm glad you told me. And I'll do my best to keep you out of it when I speak to Lila. I know she's your friend and I don't want to get you in trouble with her. So you'd better scoot before she comes home, or she'll know something's up."

"She's not exactly my friend," Val said, picking up her bike. "We're in some of the same classes, but that's about it. Lila doesn't like me very much and I — well, I don't like her very much, either." It was a hard thing to say to someone's sister. "And she's mad at me already, so it doesn't much matter whether you mention my name or not."

Lauren smiled a little. "No, I guess you're not the kind of girl Lila would choose for a friend. From what I can tell, to be a member of my sister's crowd, your folks have to be filthy rich, and your main interests in life have to be clothes, money, and boys, not necessarily in that order." She sighed. "Lila's not really a bad person. Mom and Dad have just spoiled her rotten. She's the baby of the family — our oldest brother, Dave, is a senior in college, and our sister, Lillian, lives with her husband in California. Lila's always been able to twist our parents around her little finger. But this time she's not going to get away with it, not if I can help it. Thanks for coming by, Val. I'll call you over the weekend and tell you what I find out."

Val got onto her bike. "Okay. It was nice seeing you again, Lauren. I'm glad you haven't changed!"

"Changed?" Lauren repeated. "What do you mean?"

"Nothing," Val said hastily. " 'Bye!" With a wave of her hand, she took off down Eastview Place. As she rounded the corner by the little park, a car passed her going in the opposite direction. Looking over her shoulder, Val saw it screech to a halt in front of the Bascombes' house. Lila got out.

"Thanks for the lift, Rhett," she heard Lila call. "See you tomorrow, Jeff."

The car roared away, and Val pedaled faster. Would Lauren get the truth out of Lila? she wondered. And what *was* the truth, anyway? It certainly seemed that Lila had let the Willard boys "borrow" the car, even though Toby would say that there was no real proof.

She looked at her watch. It was only four o'clock. If she hurried, she could catch him at Animal Inn before he went home and tell him all about it. And then maybe she'd have time for a short ride on The Ghost before supper.

Chapter
7

But Toby wasn't at Animal Inn when Val arrived and neither was Doc. When Val asked Pat, Doc's receptionist, where her father was, she told her that Mr. Rudisill's prize ram had come down with infectious pneumonia. Mr. Rudisill had called in a panic because he was afraid his whole herd would catch it. There were no patients waiting to see Doc whose appointments couldn't be rescheduled, so he and Toby had taken off to tend to the sick ram.

"Nothing much for you to do, Vallie," Pat said. "I've just been sitting here for the past half hour, working on this sweater I'm knitting for my little granddaughter." She held up her work. "Aren't the colors pretty? Tiffany looks so sweet in lavender and blue."

"I'm sure she'll love it," Val said. "If there's nothing for me to do, maybe I could take The Ghost out for a while. I've been neglecting him lately because I've been trying to find out who hit that collie — the one I used to call Rex."

Pat's face fell. "Oh, yes, Doc told me. Belonged to an Amish family, didn't he? That's too bad." She made a little "tcch, tcch" noise as she went back to her knitting.

"Well," said Val, "guess I'll saddle up The Ghost. I won't be gone long."

"You go right ahead," Pat said. "Real quiet day today. If Doc's not back by five-thirty, he said to tell you to go on home." She checked her watch. "That's about an hour. I'll be leaving then, too."

Val headed for The Ghost's stall in the Large Animal Clinic, stopping on the way to pick up the saddle and bridle she would use. The Ghost stuck his head out and whickered when he saw her.

"Well, Ghost," she said, giving him a kiss on his velvety nose and scratching him between his soft gray ears, "How about a ride?" As she put on his saddle and bridle, she talked to her horse like a friend. "I want to tell you about Rex. Remember Rex? He's the dog who got hit by a car."

The Ghost butted his head gently against Val's chest.

"His name isn't really Rex, but I can't help thinking about him as Rex. He died yesterday. Oh, it wasn't Dad's fault. Dad did everything he could to save him, but sometimes even Dad can't help an animal who's in real bad shape." She leaned her head against The Ghost's warm, dappled neck. "I

85

think I know who was driving the car that killed him, Ghost. And it wasn't Lauren, I'm positive of that. Lauren's okay. But Lila — well, Lila's another story. I'll tell you about Lila on our ride."

Val patted the big gray horse. "You're all set. It's a beautiful day. We'll have a great ride!"

But somehow talking to The Ghost, even while they ambled down the country lanes behind Animal Inn, wasn't the same as talking to a person who could actually talk back. Val couldn't help feeling kind of low.

"More than anything in the world I want to be a vet like Dad," she told The Ghost. It was getting dark now. The days were getting so much shorter. "But I want to save every single animal! Only I know it's not possible. But I keep thinking about Amos — he's the little boy whose dog Rex — *Luke* — was. And he's so unhappy. I want to give Luke back to him, but I can't. And maybe Lauren will forget about him, and I never even told her that I thought Amos might like a new puppy!"

The Ghost snorted and tossed his head. The air was fresh and cool, and The Ghost was eager to run. Val loosened the reins and let him trot. As they made their way back to Animal Inn, Val wondered if Lauren had talked to Lila. And if she had, what had Lila said? Lauren had told her she'd let her know what happened. But what if she forgot? Would anyone care except Val?

When Val came home, she found Teddy and Erin in the living room. Teddy was curled up on the sofa, Frank snuggled in his arms. He looked miserable.

"What's wrong?" Val asked, but Teddy didn't answer.

"Those ferret farm people called today," Erin said. "They're going to take Frank and they want Daddy to bring him out there on Sunday. I told them to call Daddy at Animal Inn and arrange it with him. Teddy's been sulking ever since."

"I am *not* sulking!" Teddy muttered, close to tears.

"He'll be happy there, Teddy," Val said, sitting next to him and stroking Frank's smooth head. Frank reached up one small paw and wrapped it around one of her fingers. Cleveland was sitting under Doc's favorite chair, glaring at the ferret with narrowed yellow eyes instead of leaping into Val's lap as he usually did. Val leaned down and called to him, but Cleveland just stared at her and didn't move. His tail was lashing, though. Val knew that meant he was mad. And Jocko and Sunshine were sulking, too.

"Frank's *not* a weasel," Teddy choked out. "It's

all because of Mrs. Racer! She *hates* Frank!"

"I'm not so crazy about him, either," said Erin. "Dandy hasn't sung a note since Frank knocked down his cage."

"Good!" Teddy said. "He made too much noise anyway."

Erin glowered at him. "Maybe we ought to give *you* to the ferret farm, too!"

"Teddy, Erin, stop that right now!" Val snapped. She felt sorry for Teddy because she knew how fond he was of Frank, and she understood how upset Erin was about her beloved canary, but she hated it when her little brother and sister bickered like this. Doc was much better at handling them than she was, but Doc hadn't gotten home yet. Mrs. Racer had left, too. To change the subject, she asked, "What's for supper, Erin?"

"Fried ferret!" Erin shouted and stomped out of the room.

"You're gonna get it, Erin," Teddy yelled. Then he burst into tears, clutching Frank closer.

"Oh, stop it!" Val said angrily. "What's the matter with everybody around here, anyway?" She went into the kitchen, closely followed by Cleveland. Jocko immediately dashed after the cat, and Sunshine chased Jocko, barking happily. Cleveland scooted between Val's feet and leaped up onto the kitchen counter, knocking a plate of Mrs. Racer's wonderful oatmeal-raisin-nut cookies to the floor. The plate broke. The dogs started gobbling the cookies faster than Val could pick them up.

"Jocko! Sunshine! Cut that out!" Val cried. Jocko looked up at her guiltily, and trotted into the dining room, but not before he'd managed to snatch another cookie. Sunshine quickly hid under the kitchen table, his nose between his paws, looking innocent.

Val started gathering up the pieces of the broken plate and promptly cut her finger. It started bleeding like crazy. She raced to the sink and ran cold water on it, noticing out of the corner of her eye that Cleveland was dipping his paw into a glass of milk on the counter and daintily licking it off.

"Cleveland!" Val wailed.

Cleveland wasn't used to being yelled at. He backed away, and the glass of milk fell over. Cleveland leaped to the floor, avoiding the lake of milk, and dashed past Val through the door to the basement. Sucking on her injured finger, Val grabbed a sponge to mop up the mess.

Just then Teddy came into the kitchen with the ferret coiled around his neck.

"You don't care about Frank," he said, sniffling. "Nobody cares about Frank but me. I thought you loved animals so much, Vallie. Aren't you *sad* that Frank has to go to the ferret farm where he won't know anybody and he won't have any friends?"

Val's finger hurt. She was tired and irritable and her patience was at an end.

"He'll have lots of friends, Teddy — ferret friends. At least he's *alive!* You should have seen that little Amish boy. His dog was dead, and he was real sad, but he didn't cry hardly at all! And he's a year younger than you."

Teddy looked away. His tear-stained cheeks were bright pink.

"He didn't cry, huh?" he mumbled into Frank's fur.

"Just a little," Val said. She wrung out the sponge into the sink. "He was very brave."

"Well, I'm brave, too," Teddy told her. "Only I love Frank, and he *isn't* dead, so I don't see why I can't keep him."

"You can't keep him, Teddy, because I say so."

Doc had come into the kitchen, and now he rested a hand on the Phillies baseball cap that Teddy always wore. There had been so much going on that Val hadn't heard him come in. He looked tired.

"We talked about this last night, remember?" Doc said. "And I told you that we have enough pets. I also reminded you that we have rules in this family, and one of those rules is that we don't adopt a pet unless everyone agrees. In this case, everyone doesn't agree. Did you feed the dogs tonight, Teddy?"

Teddy shook his head. "I kind of forgot. I was playing with Frank."

"I don't think they're very hungry, Dad," Val said, looking at the few cookies that remained.

Doc took in the situation with one glance. "Teddy, feed the dogs. Vallie, put some antiseptic on that finger. Where's Erin?"

"She's upstairs," Teddy said. "She said we were having *fried ferret* for supper! Sometimes I wish Erin wasn't my sister."

"There's not much you can do about that, now, is there?" Doc said with a slight smile. "And Frank doesn't look fried to me. Feed him, too. And tell your sister that supper's almost ready."

Teddy dumped dry dog food into Jocko's and Sunshine's bowls, then trudged out of the room, the picture of misery.

Val opened the refrigerator and took out lettuce, tomatoes, cucumbers, and bean sprouts. Doc got the big wooden salad bowl from a cupboard and then brought out oil, vinegar, and herbs from the pantry.

"Antiseptic, Vallie," Doc reminded her, and Val obediently dabbed some first-aid cream on her cut from the emergency kit in the counter drawer. As she put on a bandage, Doc said, "Want to tell me what happened?"

Val sighed. "Oh, Teddy and Erin started arguing

about Frank, and then Teddy started to cry, and Jocko chased the cat and Cleveland knocked the cookies onto the floor and spilled the milk and I cut my finger. . . ."

Doc threw up his hands, laughing. "I'm almost sorry I asked!"

"I guess it was kind of my fault," Val admitted, shredding the lettuce into the bowl. "I just got so mad at Teddy, making such a fuss because he can't keep the ferret, when Amos was so brave about Luke *dying.*"

"It wasn't your fault, Vallie," Doc said. He put a tomato on the slicing board and began cutting it up. "Teddy's upset because he can't keep Frank, and I'm sorry. But that's the way it is. I spoke to the people from the ferret farm today. They're perfectly willing to take Frank, and I told them we'd bring him there on Sunday. They're very nice people. Teddy can visit Frank any time he wants. I haven't had a chance to tell him that. It may make him feel a little better about things. Cucumber, please."

Val handed him a cucumber.

"Any luck with finding out who might have hit Luke?" Doc asked as he sliced the cucumber.

"Yes," Val said. "I saw Lauren Bascombe today. It's her car, all right, but she wasn't driving it Tuesday because she was shopping in Philadelphia with her mother. She thinks Lila may have let Jeff Willard's older brother drive it. She's really furious at Lila."

Doc glanced up from his cucumber. "Do I detect a note of satisfaction about that?"

"Well. . . ." Val sprinkled some bean sprouts over the lettuce and tomatoes. "I don't like Lila very much. You know that. Lila's not a very nice person."

"And you wouldn't mind seeing her get into trouble, is that it?"

"Oh, Dad!" Val opened the freezer compartment of the refrigerator and took out a plastic bag of lima beans that Mrs. Racer had frozen. She dropped them into a saucepan, and added a little water. She didn't know how to answer.

"Don't forget what's really important, Vallie," Doc said quietly. "What's really important is to make the person who was responsible for the dog's death realize what he's done. What's *not* important is being pleased that someone you don't like is going to have a hard time."

"But Lila smashed my dog!" Val cried. "In art yesterday, I was making this really nice clay figure of Luke, and when I told Lila that Toby thought it was Lauren's car that hit him — the *real* Luke — she just squooshed it!"

"Could you fix it?" Doc asked.

"Yes. I fixed it," Val admitted. "On Monday we're going to put our ceramics in the kiln. I'll always have something to remember Luke by."

"So what Lila did didn't matter at all, did it?"

"I guess not," Val said.

"Then don't be vindictive. Do you know what that means?"

"I think so," Val replied slowly. "It means . . . being mad at somebody and wanting something bad to happen to them because they deserve it."

Doc dropped the cucumbers into the salad, took up the wooden fork and spoon, and mixed everything together. "Something like that. It's not a good thing to be. Remember that, Vallie."

"But, Dad," Val said, sitting down on the tall wooden stool behind the counter, "if Lila really *did* let Jeff and his brother borrow Lauren's car, which she shouldn't have done, and if they really *did* hit Luke, then it's her fault as much as theirs, isn't it? And she shouldn't be allowed to get away with it, should she? So she *does* deserve to have Lauren — and me — mad at her! I don't see where that's being vindictive."

"Honey, if that's what actually happened — and you don't know that it is, remember — it's up to Lila's family, and Jeff and Rhett's as well, to make them understand that what they did was wrong," Doc said. "You've done everything you could. Now it's up to them."

"I guess you're right," Val sighed. "Only Lila is such a *pig!* It's not fair that Luke died because of her.

She doesn't care about him at all. And Jeff's just as bad! You should have heard them yesterday. I know," she added hastily, "I shouldn't have been eavesdropping. But I couldn't help overhearing what they were saying. It didn't make a whole lot of sense at first, because I couldn't hear everything, but I could tell that they both had something to do with the accident, and neither of them cared one single bit! I bet they wouldn't even have felt sorry if they'd seen Amos Gebhart's face when he found out his dog was dead!"

Doc reached out and stroked her cheek, then took her chin in his hand, forcing her to meet his eyes. "Vallie, you want to be a vet when you grow up, and that makes me very, very proud. But a vet can't change the world. All we can do is try to cure sick animals and make people aware that animal life is important, too. Some people know that already. Others will never, ever learn, no matter how hard we try to convince them. Lila — and Jeff and Rhett — may be some of those 'others.' I know it hurts, honey, but that's the way it is."

"Isn't dinner ready yet?"

Erin came into the kitchen, sniffing the air.

"Oh, Vallie, is the casserole burning? Something smells disgusting! Hi, Daddy. I didn't know you were home." She kissed Doc and gave him a hug.

Val leaped off her stool and turned off the burner

under the pot of lima beans. "I did it again!" she moaned, lifting the lid and peering at the shriveled gray-green vegetables stuck to the bottom of the pan.

"Yuck! That's really gross," Erin said. "Vallie, let's face it. You will *never* be a great cook." She wriggled out of Doc's embrace and took a serving bowl from under the counter. "Quick — dump the limas in here. If we add some butter, and salt and pepper, they'll be okay. Just don't tell Teddy they got burned. If we don't tell him, he'll never notice."

"What won't I notice?"

Teddy and Frank poked their heads into the kitchen. Frank's eyes were as beady and bright as ever. Teddy's were red and swollen from tears.

"Vallie burned the limas again," Erin said cheerfully. "We didn't want to tell you because you're such a lima bean freak. They'll taste just fine."

"I won't eat burned lima beans," Teddy said. "I bet Frank won't, either!"

"Teddy," Doc said, "you don't have to eat the lima beans. Neither does Frank. Now how about a smile?"

Teddy scowled. "I don't feel like smiling. I'm mad at you. You won't let me keep Frank."

"No, I won't," Doc agreed, "and I've explained why. By the way, I have a message for you from Toby."

"You do?" Teddy brightened just a little. He liked Toby a lot.

"Toby says to tell you that he talked to the Detwilers — the ferret farm people, remember? — and they want you to know that you can visit Frank whenever you like until he finds a permanent home. Toby's going with us on Sunday, too. He's never been to the ferret farm, and he's looking forward to it."

Teddy brightened even more. "Really? That's pretty neat. On the way back, could we maybe go to Curran's Dairy for some ice cream?" he asked hopefully. "I'll probably be feeling pretty sad after I say good-bye to good ol' Frank, and ice cream always cheers me up."

"I think that could be arranged," Doc said, smiling.

"Can we eat now?" Teddy asked. "I'm starvin' like Marvin!"

"After you put Frank up in your room," Doc said. "And make sure you close the door tight so he doesn't get out."

"Okay," Teddy said. He ran out of the kitchen, and Val heard him say to the ferret, "I guess it won't be so bad after all. And I'll visit you every single chance I get. . . ."

Erin, who was putting supper on the kitchen table, suddenly paused by the door to the dining room and cocked her head, listening. Her face lit up.

"Do you hear that?" she asked Val and Doc.

They listened, too. Very faintly, they heard a cascade of trills, chirps, and warbles.

"It's Dandy! He's singing!" Erin cried.

Chapter
8

Val had hoped that Lauren might call that night to tell her what she had found out after talking to Lila. She didn't even phone Jill because she didn't want the line to be busy if Lauren tried to call, but Lauren didn't. Val considered calling Lauren, then decided against it. If Lila answered, she certainly didn't want to speak to her.

The next morning, Saturday, Val woke up early as usual, after a restless night. Saturdays she worked all day at Animal Inn. Ever since she had bought The Ghost, she left the house about an hour before Doc did so she could ride her horse before office hours began. After a quick breakfast of granola and milk, and orange juice, Val tucked an apple and some carrots into the pockets of her jacket for The Ghost and took off on her bike.

It was a beautiful, bright, frosty morning. Val could see her breath as she rode along. The unseasonably warm weather seemed to have broken at last. On the porches of some of the houses she passed on her way, Val noticed big orange pumpkins and corn shocks, and a couple of "pumpkin people" — clothing stuffed with straw, like scarecrows, with pumpkin heads painted with funny faces.

The Taylors hadn't gotten their pumpkins yet. Maybe they could buy some on their way home from the ferret farm tomorrow. They always bought three: one for Teddy, one for Erin, and one for Val. Every year they tried to outdo each other in cutting the best jack o' lantern. Erin was usually the winner. She was very artistic, and spent hours carefully carving her pumpkin's features. Teddy's wasn't as fancy, but it was always the scariest. Val carved the same face each year, a classic jack o'lantern with triangular eyes and nose and a big gap-toothed grin. I wonder if I'm too old to make a jack o'lantern this year, Val thought. But then she decided she wasn't. Maybe she'd carve a different face this time, though, just for variety.

Val suddenly remembered the Harvest Dance. She hadn't thought about it at all since Luke had been hit, and it was less than a week away. Val had been looking forward to it, but now it didn't seem like much fun. Lila would figure out some way to make Val uncomfortable, she was sure. Maybe I just won't go, she thought. But she'd planned to go with Jill, and Jill wouldn't let her stay home. Besides, it would look funny if she didn't show up since she was a member of the planning committee.

Val biked down Orchard Lane past Animal Inn's Small Animal Clinic and coasted to a stop by the barn. Mike Strickler came out just then, a broad grin on his face.

"Figured you'd be showing up right around now," he said cheerfully. "I was just tellin' The Ghost, 'Vallie'll be here any minute, and I bet she's got some treats for you, too.' He seemed mighty glad to hear that."

"Everything okay with the patients?" Val asked.

"Sure, everything's okay. Don't I check on 'em all every couple of hours through the night? Had a nice long talk with that there billy goat," he told her. "And you know what he said?"

Val couldn't help smiling. "What did he say?"

"He said, real confidential-like, that goats don't really eat tin cans like people think." He paused for effect. "They like old tires much better — easier to digest."

Val laughed. "I'll remember that, Mike. If I find an old tire lying around, I'll make sure Scruffy gets first crack at it."

Mike ambled off to finish cleaning out the stalls, and Val went in to say good-morning to The Ghost. After she'd given him the apple, she saddled him up, and soon they were off at a brisk trot. The Ghost was as frisky as a colt, and Val had a hard time preventing him from breaking into a gallop. When they returned to the barn at last, Val felt as though all the cobwebs had been blown out of her head by the brisk, crisp air.

"I guess Dad's right about me not being able to do anything else about Luke," she said to The Ghost as she fed him the carrots one by one. "Even if Lauren doesn't call me, I'll find out sooner or later. Lila won't be shy about telling me, that's for sure!"

The big gray horse nodded just as if he'd understood.

When she had taken off his saddle and bridle and finished rubbing him down, Val put his halter on him and led him out to the pasture behind the barn. Closing the gate after he was safely inside, she gave him an affectionate pat on the rump and watched in loving admiration as he trotted off, tossing his head and capering like a two-year-old rather than the middle-aged gentleman he actually was. And to think that Mr. Merrill had actually intended to have him destroyed!

"At least I saved *your* life, Ghost," Val said aloud. "If I never do another good thing in my whole life, I'll always be proud of that."

Then she hurried off to the Small Animal Clinic. There were several cars in the parking lot already, including Doc's. It looked as though it was going to be a busy day at Animal Inn.

* * *

And it was. It seemed that all the pet owners in Essex, Pennsylvania, had decided to bring their injured or ailing animals to Doc Taylor on that bright October Saturday. Val, Toby, and Doc were so busy, they hardly had time to grab a bite of lunch. Dogs, cats, hamsters, gerbils, even a pet raccoon, were tended, treated, and sent on their way. A cocker spaniel with a bad ear infection and a white rat with a nasty case of ringworm were admitted to the small animal infirmary; a cat whose tail had been broken when someone had accidentally closed a door on it was treated and sent home; a dog went into convulsions in the waiting room, scaring everybody half to death; and on, and on, and on.

Things had finally begun to quiet down around three o'clock, and Val was sitting behind the reception desk having a brief and well-deserved rest, when the outside door opened for what seemed like the thousandth time that day.

Val looked up and, to her surprise, saw Lauren Bascombe.

"Lauren! Hi," she cried, coming out from behind the desk. "What did you find out?"

"Plenty," Lauren said. She glanced around the waiting room at the two people who were waiting

103

for Doc to examine their pets. "Is there some place we can talk in private?"

"Sure. Just let me get Toby. He can take over for me for a few minutes here," said Val. She found Toby in the infirmary, and after Val had introduced him to Lauren, he took Val's place. "I'll be right back," she promised.

"Let's go outside," Lauren suggested. "I have something to show you."

Val followed her out of Animal Inn and Lauren led the way to the white Corvette.

"Take a look at the passenger seat," Lauren instructed with a little smile.

Val peered into the car through the open window, and gave a squeal of delight. There, snuggled down on a soft blue cushion in a big wicker basket was the most adorable collie puppy she had ever seen. Bright brown eyes looked back at her out of a little ball of gold-and-white fur.

"Oh, Lauren!" Val cried. "For Amos?"

Lauren nodded. "It's a present from Lila, Jeff, and Rhett."

"But how. . . . When — ?" Val stammered.

"I'll tell you the 'when' first," Lauren said. "The minute Lila got home yesterday, I sat her down, and made her tell me the truth. And believe me, it wasn't easy! But finally she admitted that she'd given Rhett my keys, and he and Jeff had gone for a joyride

104

Tuesday afternoon. She says she didn't know that they'd hit the dog until you told her about the accident."

"I'm sure that's true," Val said, "because of what I heard her and Jeff saying in the cafeteria."

"Lila begged and pleaded with me not to tell Mother and Daddy," Lauren went on, "but there was no way I was going to agree to sweep everything under the rug this time. I've covered up for her too many times already. When they got home, I told Daddy and Mother the whole story, and they drove Lila right straight over to the Willards'. To make a long story short, both Jeff and Rhett are grounded for three weeks, and so is Lila. And the three of them have to pool their allowances to pay for this little guy here." She nodded at the puppy. "I went to Harrisburg with Lila and Daddy this morning to buy him. He has a pedigree longer than *he* is, and he cost enough to prove it, so it's going to take a lot of allowances for those kids to pay Daddy back." Lauren grinned. "I guess that pretty much covers the 'how,' too."

"Oh, Lauren, thank you!" Val said. "If anything can cheer Amos up, this puppy will. Are you going to take him to the Gebharts' farm now? I can get driving directions from my father. I'd give anything to see Amos's face when you give him the puppy."

"You will," Lauren told her, smiling. "That's

why I brought Luke Junior here to Animal Inn. I thought maybe you'd like to deliver him yourself, if Doc doesn't mind driving you there after the office closes."

"Really? Oh, Lauren, thank you," Val said again. It was all she could think of to say. Then suddenly she added, "You're just as nice as I always thought you were! I never really believed that you'd be a hit-and-run driver, honest."

"Thank *you*," said Lauren. "I only hope Lila and the Willard boys have learned their lesson," She sighed. "I suppose it's partly my fault that Lila's the way she is. I've helped spoil her as much as anyone else in the family."

"I guess Lila's pretty furious at me, isn't she?" Val asked.

"You are not exactly my little sister's favorite person at the moment," Lauren admitted. "But don't let that bother you. You did the right thing, and that's all that matters."

Lauren looked at her watch, "Listen, Val, I have to go. You take Luke Junior, and I'll bring in the basket. Oh, and the kennel gave me a sheet of instructions on how to take care of him and enough food for a week. He's only three months old, so he has to be fed often — but you know all about that, and probably Amos and his folks do, too. He's had all his puppy shots, and he's super healthy."

Lauren opened the car door, and Val gently picked

up the puppy. It wriggled happily in her arms and licked her face with its little pink tongue. Lauren followed her back into Animal Inn with the basket.

"Hey, where did you get that?" Toby asked as they entered. "What a neat little guy!"

"Lauren brought him for Amos," Val told him happily. "Lila and the Willard boys are paying for him out of their allowances. And guess what, Toby! Lauren says I can give him to Amos myself! You want to come, too? Dad can drive us to the Gebharts' after work."

"Gee, yeah, that'd be great," Toby said. "Can I hold him for a minute?"

"Sure," said Val. "Just be very careful. He's only a baby."

Toby shot her a disdainful look. "I've taken care of puppies all my life. Of course I'll be careful." He took Luke Junior from Val and cuddled him under his chin.

"Well, it looks like everything's under control," said Lauren. " 'Bye, Val, Toby. And Val, say hi to Doc for me. I haven't seen him in a long time." She patted the puppy's head. "Be a good boy, Junior."

After Lauren had left, Val said to Toby, "She didn't change, Toby. Going to college and getting a fancy car didn't change Lauren Bascombe one bit!"

"That's good," Toby said. "It's funny, you know?"

"What's funny?"

"It's funny that two sisters can be so different. Wouldn't you think that some of Lauren's niceness would rub off on Lila?"

"Maybe it will one of these days," Val said. Then she made a wry face. "But not right away. I have a feeling Lila's going to do her best to get back at me for this. I'm not looking forward to seeing her on Monday morning."

"I don't guess she likes me very much, either," Toby said. "But that doesn't matter, because I *don't* have to see her Monday morning." He glanced down at the puppy in his arms, then thrust it at Val. "Here. You can have him back. He just wet all over my shirt!"

Laughing, Val took Luke Junior and put him back into his cushioned basket. He immediately curled up into a furry ball and dropped off to sleep.

"You keep an eye on him," she told Toby. "I'm going to go tell Doc. He'll be as happy as we are!"

The last patient had been taken care of, and the treatment rooms and waiting room had been cleaned up. Doc, Toby, and Val — carrying the puppy — piled into Doc's car and headed for the Gebharts' farm. As Mrs. Racer had said, it was near her son Henry's place, so they had no difficulty finding it.

Doc pulled up in front of the house. It was a big brick farmhouse with two front doors. Lots of bright yellow and orange marigolds and chrysanthemums were blooming in the yard, though Val couldn't see them very well because it was getting dark. The windows were all lighted. It looked like a warm and friendly place.

Val got out of the car and went up onto the porch. Then she hesitated. Which door should she knock on? She decided on the left one, and rapped on the panel. A moment later, the door opened, and a woman in Amish dress smiled at Val, though she looked surprised to see her.

"Mrs. Gebhart?" Val asked.

"That's right. Can I help you?" the woman replied.

"You don't know me, but I'm Valentine Taylor," Val began. "My father's out in the car. He's Doctor Theodore Taylor, from Animal Inn, where your collie was taken after he got hit by a car. Is Amos home? Because we have something for him!"

"Well, my goodness," said Mrs. Gebhart. "Come on in. I'll get Amos. He's out back, by the pear tree. That's where we buried Luke. Amos sits out there a lot now."

Val followed her into the hall and waited while Mrs. Gebhart went to the back door. "Amos, there's somebody to see you," she called, then returned and said to Val, "Would you like to come into the parlor?"

109

"No, thanks," Val said. "I'll wait here if you don't mind."

Amos came in then, his face solemn. When he saw Val, his eyes widened, but he didn't say anything.

"This here girl's from the place where they took care of Luke," his mother told him. "Say howdy, Amos."

"Howdy," Amos said obediently. But he didn't smile.

"Amos, will you come outside with me?" Val asked. "There's a surprise for you in my dad's car."

"A surprise?" Amos echoed, looking puzzled. "What kind of surprise?"

"Follow me and you'll find out," Val told him.

The little boy trotted after her — and stopped in his tracks when he saw Toby standing on the porch with the basket and the puppy in his arms.

"Oh!" said Amos, almost in a whisper.

"He's for you, Amos," Val said. "I know he can't really take Luke's place, but he's an awfully nice puppy."

"He's for me?" Amos echoed. "Honest?"

"Well now, I don't know . . ." said Mrs. Gebhart. "You didn't have to go and buy Amos another dog. It wasn't your fault Luke died."

"Oh, but it's not from us," Val said quickly. "It's from the people whose car hit Luke. They felt awful about it, and so they bought this puppy and asked us to bring it to Amos." That wasn't exactly true, but in a case like this, Val figured a white lie wouldn't do any harm. "They'll feel even worse if Amos can't keep him."

Amos had gone over to the basket, which Toby had set down on the floor of the porch. He kneeled down and patted the puppy's furry head, and Luke Junior began eagerly licking his hand. Slowly, a smile spread over the little boy's solemn face. He looked up at his mother.

"Mom, I think he likes me! Can I keep him? He can be my friend, like Luke was!"

Mrs. Gebhart smiled, too. "I guess maybe you can. But you better ask your pop first."

"Pop! Pop, guess what! The Animal Inn people brought me a puppy," Amos shouted as he dashed off to find his father. Toby and Val looked at each other and grinned. Seconds later, Amos came running back, beaming. "Pop says okay!" He dropped to his knees again beside the puppy and picked it up very gently and carefully, laughing as it licked his face. "Thank you! Thank you very, very much!" he said to Val. "Does he have a name?"

"Not exactly," Val said. "We've been calling him Luke Junior, but you can call him anything you like."

"Not Luke," Amos said at once, shaking his

head. "There'll never be another Luke. I'll have to think of a new name."

"You know, Amos, before we found out Luke's real name, we called him Rex," Val said. "It means 'king.' "

"Rex," Amos repeated thoughtfully. "Rex is a good name for a dog. That's what I'll call him. And when he grows up, he'll be big and strong, just like a king!"

Val sighed happily. It was worth having Lila mad at her for the rest of her life, to see Amos's smile.

Chapter
9

Rock music blared over the loudspeakers in the gaily decorated gym of Hamilton Junior High. It was Friday night, and the Harvest Dance was in full swing. Boys and girls in jeans were dancing up a storm, and Val and Toby were in the midst of them.

"I didn't know you were such a terrific dancer," Val shouted over the music to Toby.

"There's a lot you don't know about me," he shouted back. "You didn't know I knew how to drive, either. Besides, there's nothing to it. You just shuffle your feet a lot and wave your arms around in time to the music. Anybody can do that."

Val giggled. "Guess you're right, at that. I've got two left feet, but they both seem to be working all right for once."

The number ended with a screech of guitars and an earsplitting drumroll. The dancers all yelled and applauded, then headed for the refreshment tables. Val's committee had provided piles of cookies, pretzels, and potato chips, and gallons of cider. As she and Toby joined the crowd, Val told him, "If you want some of Mrs. Racer's cookies, you'd better get them now. They're going fast."

Toby reached out one long arm and snatched a handful from a paper plate. "Got 'em!" he announced cheerfully. "Mrs. Racer ought to open a bakery. She'd be a millionaire if she started selling this stuff." He took a big bite of a peanut-butter-chocolate-chip cookie. Val managed to pour some cider into two paper cups, and they moved out of the way of other hungry dancers to a part of the gym that wasn't so crowded.

"You know," Toby said, "this dance hasn't turned out to be nearly as bad as I thought it was going to be."

Val gave him a dirty look. "Thanks a bunch! Why did you come if you thought it was going to be so terrible?"

Toby shrugged. "Well, you said it was a fund-raiser so the school could buy some new athletic equipment, and that sounded like a good cause. Besides, I thought I ought to be around to protect you from Lila."

"In that case, you're out of luck," Val said. "Lila's not here. Remember, I told you she's been grounded for three weeks, and so has Jeff Willard. And Jeff's big brother, Rhett, isn't allowed to drive a car for two whole months."

"Yeah, that's right. Has Lila been getting on your case at school this week?" Toby asked, biting into another cookie.

"Has she ever!" Val said with a sigh. "None of the girls in her crowd are supposed to speak to me — not that I care. They've never been very friendly anyway. But it really burned me up when Courtney deliberately spilled grape soda all over my science notes in the cafeteria the other day. That was right after Kimberly switched her hamburger for my veggieburger. I almost ate *meat*!" She shuddered at the memory. "And then yesterday, Lila tripped me when I was going up to speak to Mr. Steele in English class. I fell flat on my face. Boy, was I embarrassed! Lila laughed like anything, but Mr. Steele told her it wasn't funny, and to keep her feet under her chair where they belonged. I skinned my knee — it still kind of hurts."

"That sounds like grade school stuff, not junior high," Toby said contemptuously. "She's really the pits!"

"Hi, Val, Toby. How you doing? Having fun?" Jill asked, coming over to where Val and Toby were standing.

"Not bad," said Toby. "The cookies are great. Want one?"

"No, thanks. But you're right — they're delicious." She grinned at him. "Is that the only

115

thing you like about the Harvest Dance?"

"Well, I like dancing, but I guess I like eating better," Toby admitted. "I'm glad you asked me to come, Val. The kids at Hamilton are okay. I thought they'd be stuck-up, like Lila, but they're not."

"I'm having a super time," Jill told them. "Everybody says this is the most successful Harvest Dance the school's ever had. We made lots of money, too. Now we can buy new uniforms for the basketball team, and maybe there'll be enough left over for some equipment for the girls' softball team. But the very best part is that Lila Bascombe's sitting at home, eating her heart out!"

Val grinned. "I have to admit that's a definite plus, but Dad would say I'm being vindictive again."

"Where is Doc?" Toby asked. "I haven't seen him since the dance started. For a chaperone, he's keeping a pretty low profile."

"He's right over there, talking to my science teacher, Ms. Lessing," said Val.

Toby looked where she was pointing. "That's a pretty neat science teacher," he said admiringly. "You should see the old guy who teaches science at Kennedy. He looks like a cross between a turtle and a toad."

"Yuck!" Jill said with a giggle. "I'm glad I go to Hamilton. I hate science, but Ms. Lessing's really nice. She's pretty, too."

Val caught her father's eye and waved. A few minutes later, he weaved his way through the crowd to her side. Putting an arm around her shoulders, he said, "If they'd play some *real* music, I'd ask you to dance, Vallie, but all that leaping around would probably land me in the hospital." He turned to Toby. "You were looking pretty good out there, young man. I didn't realize that dancing was another of your talents."

Toby's ears turned red. "It's like I told Val — you just keep everything moving, and you look like you know what you're doing," he said.

A sudden blast of music told everyone that the disc jockey was back on the job, and Jill grabbed Toby's hand. "C'mon, Toby," she urged. "You haven't danced with me yet. Want to give it a try?"

"Sure — why not?" Toby allowed himself to be dragged off by Jill, calling over his shoulder, "See you later, Val, Doc."

"Everything okay?" Doc asked, smiling down at Val.

"Everything's great," she told him, smiling back. "The dance is a big success, and I'm so glad that Toby's here, and that you are, too. And I'm *super* glad that Amos has a new puppy and that Teddy isn't sad anymore about Frank. . . ."

"But?" Doc prodded.

"But — well, I'm *not* happy that Lila's so mad at me. I guess it's not very nice, but I'm glad she's not here tonight," Val confessed.

"You know something, Vallie? I'm glad, too," Doc said. "You don't have to feel guilty about that. Maybe Lila's learned something from all this."

"That's what Lauren said," Val told him. "But I have a feeling she's not going to let me forget about it for a long, long time."

"Hi, Val. Hi, Doctor Taylor." Nancy Fox, a member of Val's refreshment committee, came up to her. "Listen, Val, do you think you could take over for me at the cookie table for a little while? Oh, and Sarah says they're all out of cider, and is there any more? And Chuck was bringing in the last box of pretzels from the locker room, but he tripped and fell, and they're all broken into a million pieces. I'm going to take Tammy's place because she has a stomachache and she's going home. . . ."

"Okay, okay!" Val said, laughing. "Don't worry about it — I'll take care of everything."

Nancy hurried off, and Val gave her father a quick kiss on the cheek. "Gotta run. Oh, Dad, would you mind helping Tommy bring out the rest of the cider jugs? They're in the girls' locker room — knock before you go in! See you later." And she dashed off to take up her duties.

The next day at Animal Inn was busy, as usual, and Val had a hard time keeping her eyes open for most of it. She and Doc hadn't gotten home until after eleven o'clock the night before — they had stayed to help clean up the gym after the dance and then had driven Toby to the Currans' farm. Toby was a little bleary-eyed, too, though he insisted that he never went to bed much before eleven anyway.

Doc closed the office promptly at five that afternoon, and for once he and Val went straight back to the house without having to stop off and tend to a patient on the way. Val was looking forward to a good supper, some TV, and going to bed early. Her hand was on the front doorknob, when suddenly the door was flung open by Teddy.

"It's about time!" he shouted. "I thought you were *never* coming home! Vallie, guess what! Dad, you'll never guess what happened!"

"No, we probably won't unless you tell us," Doc said, giving him a hug and a kiss. "What's up?"

"Listen," Teddy said, his eyes sparkling under the visor of his Phillies baseball cap.

Val and Doc obediently stood still and listened. From somewhere at the back of the house, Val heard a faint cheeping sound.

"Did you hear that?" Erin asked, running into the hall.

"Yes, we heard it, all right," said Doc. "It sounds like. . . ."

"Baby chicks?" Val asked. She was hardly able to believe her ears.

"Peeps!" Teddy shouted. "Come and see!"

"They're the cutest things I ever saw," said Erin, taking Doc's hand and pulling him toward the kitchen. "Six of them — six baby chicks! Mr. Gebhart brought them this afternoon. He drove right up to the door in his buggy, and he gave Mrs. Racer lots of eggs, and then Amos came in with this box. . . ."

"Let *me* tell, Erin," Teddy said. "Amos came in with this box, like Erin said, and there were six baby chicks in it! They were peeping like anything, and they're all yellow and fluffy. They're for us! Mr. Gebhart said they'll grow up to be real good chickens, and they'll all lay lots of eggs for us. And I'm going to take care of them! Come and see!"

Numbly, Val and Doc followed Teddy and Erin into the kitchen. Mrs. Racer beamed at them. "Just look at these little fellows," she said, pointing to a big cardboard box on the kitchen table. "Leghorns, that's what they are. Leghorns are good layers. You can put 'em in the garage with the rabbits and the duck. But they'll have to stay in the house for a while, till they're older." She picked up one little fluffy yellow ball. "I know all about taking care of chickens. I'll show Teddy how to feed 'em. Now isn't this a nice little peep?"

Val grinned delightedly. "Can I hold him? Oh,

Dad, just look at him — or *her*, I guess. Isn't she adorable?"

Doc sighed. "I think this is the point where I make my speech about nobody adopting a pet unless everyone agrees, but it looks like I'm outnumbered." He looked down at the baby chick in Val's hands, then at Teddy. "Teddy, if these chicks are going to be your responsibility, that means that you have to feed them and take care of them all by yourself. And you'll have to listen to Mrs. Racer and do everything she tells you. Okay?"

Teddy nodded vigorously. "Okay! And maybe I could bring them to school for Show-and-Tell when they're a little older. And when they're a *lot* older, I can sell the eggs and make lots of money!" He turned to Val. "I think she's getting tired. I'd better put her back with the others."

Val handed the chick to Teddy. He carefully returned her to the box, then leaned over his new pets, watching as they scurried around, cheeping and pecking at the grains of mash on the bottom of the box. "Wait till I tell Eric that I have six chickens!"

"Six chickens, four rabbits, two dogs, one duck, and one cat," Doc mumbled. "Not to mention the hamsters and the canary." He glanced ruefully at Val. "Better tell Toby to make a sign for this house — ANIMAL INN ANNEX."

Val beamed. "I think that's a wonderful idea!"

Coming soon
Animal Inn #3
Monkey Business

"This monkey obviously has an upper respiratory infection," Doc told the menagerie owner. "And she appears to be undernourished. Antibiotics and good food would fix her up in no time. Why don't you bring Gigi to Animal Inn? We can give her what she needs to make her better."

"I'll do that," the man said. "Hey, you want to take a look at Little Leo? Little Leo is my lion cub. The people like him because he is cute, but now he's not so cute anymore. He just lies there. He doesn't eat, doesn't play, he doesn't do anything. You make him better, too. Okay?"

Val went over to the dirty cage where Little Leo was lying, and crouched down so she was at eye level with the animal. He was a very sad sight—so thin that Val could see all his ribs. Tears stung Val's eyes. How could anybody let a baby like this get so sick?

"I'll get my son to bring Little Leo and Gigi to your hospital and you make them well. The price does not matter."

Val and Doc looked at each other helplessly. Animal Inn was officially closed for the day. It was Doc's first day off in ages. But they couldn't turn away two animals in such desperate need as the friendly monkey and sad lion club...

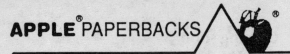